TEEN
LIS

10/10/23

Lister, Alison

No limit on love

No Limit on Love

No Limit on Love

ALISON LISTER

JAMES LORIMER & COMPANY LTD., PUBLISHERS
TORONTO

James Lorimer & Company Ltd., Publishers acknowledges funding support
from the Ontario Arts Council (OAC), an agency of the Government of
Ontario. We acknowledge the support of the Canada Council for the Arts,
which last year invested $153 million to bring the arts to Canadians throughout
the country. This project has been made possible in part by the Government of
Canada and with the support of Ontario Creates.

Cover design: Tyler Cleroux
Cover image: Shutterstock

Library and Archives Canada Cataloguing in Publication

Title: No limit on love / Alison Lister.
Names: Lister, Alison (Alison E.), author.
Identifiers: Canadiana 20220484945 | ISBN 9781459417243 (hardcover) |
    ISBN 9781459417175 (softcover) | ISBN 9781459417403 (epub)
Subjects: LCGFT: Novels.
Classification: LCC PS8623.I86 N6 2023 | DDC C813/.6—dc23

Published by: Distributed in Canada by: Distributed in the US by:
James Lorimer &   Formac Lorimer Books   Lerner Publisher Services
Company Ltd., Publishers   5502 Atlantic Street   241 1st Ave. N.
117 Peter Street, Suite 304 Halifax, NS, Canada   Minneapolis, MN, USA
Toronto, ON, Canada   B3H 1G4   55401
M5V 0M3   www.formaclorimerbooks.ca   www.lernerbooks.com
www.lorimer.ca

Printed and bound in Canada.
Manufactured by Friesens Corporation in Altona, Manitoba,
Canada in February 2023.
Job #295018

To Gray (15) and Gillian (18), my incredible
and amazing children,
who inspire and challenge me every day

01 *Powerless*

THE POWER had been out for three days by the time I
started to lose my shit. I was tired of trying to get my
data to work so I could go on Instagram and TikTok.
The apps would open, but the dreaded *COULDN'T
REFRESH FEED* kept popping up over and over.

Damn.

I wanted to see more of the destruction. I needed
to find out what this storm had done to my city.

Our three-bedroom townhome had escaped damage,

but we'd lost two of our backyard fences. The dog had to be kept inside or taken out on his leash to the front yard. It wasn't a big deal, I supposed, but it was one more thing I had to worry about, on top of school and my non-existent love life.

Fun times.

"Do you need anything charged today?" my dad asked as he got ready to go into the office. He had power at work, so he could take my laptop to charge up if I wanted him to. But what was the point? I couldn't access my Google Classroom without Wi-Fi.

"No, I'm good," I said. "Are you going to buy batteries?"

We had three camping lanterns and a radio, but my dad had forgotten to stock up on batteries for an emergency.

"I'll get some today. Hopefully. There might have been a run on them. I know it's almost impossible to find a generator these days."

"A what?"

"A generator. Some of the people in our

community are using them. They're noisy but you can power up some of the things you need in your house as long as you have gas for the generator."

"Oh! Why don't we have one?"

He sighed. "I almost bought one last year, but they're expensive. And the longest we've ever been without power was twelve hours, and that was twenty years ago."

I nodded, tossing the book I'd been reading onto the coffee table. "When do you think we'll get our power back?"

"Oh my God. Please say tonight. Please!" my brother, Jake, moaned.

"At least you have your Switch to play," I mumbled.

"Do you need it charged?" my dad asked him.

"Nah, it's good for a while."

"All right. Well, I'll see you guys later."

The dog yelped with excitement. He had followed my dad to the entryway, but couldn't get past the metal gate that kept him from running out the front door whenever it was opened.

"Oh my God, Izzy, stop!" my mom said. "Quiet!"

She lured him with a stuffed toy, and he galloped over, attacking it with an aggressive growl.

"Good boy. Get it," she said, pretending to try to take it from him.

It was a good way to distract him and get him to stop whining and yapping when people left the house. Izzy was a tad high-strung.

"I'm gonna practise my song," I said, heading upstairs. "Please pretend you can't hear me. I don't want any comments on this. I'm nervous enough."

This vocal solo would be the death of me. Maybe? I'm not sure what possessed me to take Vocal Music class this semester, but I loved to sing, and I had assumed it would focus on ensemble singing. Which it had, mostly. Except for our final assignment. We had to choose a song and sing it on our own, with accompaniment provided by the teacher on the piano. The other students in the class had been taking vocal music all through high school, whereas this was my first year, even though I was in grade eleven.

"Got it," my mom said. "Break a leg."

"That's not — " I protested.

"Jake, will you please pass me my laptop?" Mom said to my younger brother.

"Why? There's no Wi-Fi."

"No, but it's charged, so I can try to do some writing."

I rolled my eyes and climbed the stairs to my cozy room. It was sunny out, and I'd opened my curtains, so at least I could see. And I had lots of candles so when night fell, I could light one and it would look kind of nice. But I was eager for the power to be back.

There was no power at my school, so classes had been cancelled. At a different time of year that might have been a plus. But it was almost June and I had final assignments due.

Climate change. I'd seen the news and watched natural disasters hit other places, always feeling like my city was safe from anything major. Then we'd had the tornado in 2018, which hadn't affected us personally except for a twelve-hour power disruption — nothing compared to *this*. I figured we were well protected from flooding and forest fires, but because the heat and humidity tended to build on summer days, we'd had our share of storms over the years.

Now they were getting worse.

When I'd been six and scared of tornados, my mother had assured me that if any tornados ever came through this area, they would barely register on the F-Scale. She'd had to walk back those words in recent years. She admitted that things were looking bad and that when they'd had me and my brother, the predictions on climate change had sounded far-fetched and unbelievable.

What if the storms got so violent that they flattened houses instead of only taking some shingles off and blowing over trees? What if another big storm came next week that completely demolished the city? My stomach felt tight and uneasy when I thought of the future. Why couldn't I have been born in an earlier time, when the world didn't seem to be on its last legs?

We'd gotten through the worst of the COVID

pandemic, and everything seemed almost normal again — mostly. Then the trucker protest downtown, when anti-maskers and anti-vaccine folks had terrorized the core and threatened political consequences to their demands not being met. That had been hella fun. Then Russia had invaded Ukraine, and now World War III seemed to be lurking on the horizon.

Why couldn't we get a break? All I wanted to do was graduate high school and figure out where to go from there, but I didn't even know what was happening from one day to the next. Did I even have a future?

Because of free-floating anxiety and the isolation of the COVID lockdown, my parents had signed both my brother and me up for online counselling. Jake had done it twice and then declared it was useless and he had no interest. I'd found that talking to someone about what was going on actually did help, and my counsellor, Fiza, was awesome. We had our sessions in person now. She had given me tools to use to stop some of these negative thoughts when they came, or at least argue with them inside my own head. But it was hard.

How were you supposed to have positive thoughts in a world that was literally *on fire*?

At least, when I was worried about the fate of the world, I had less time to worry about other stuff. Such as how my Vocal Music class would react to the fact that I'd chosen "I'm Yours" by Jason Mraz for my solo performance. My teacher had seemed a bit confused at the fact that the song was sung by a guy, but then the lyrics didn't make reference to it, so it worked. I wouldn't have cared if they had, honestly. She'd seen the wisdom of my choice when I'd tried to sing a song in a higher key. I sang alto when the class performed as a group. There were only two boys in the class who sang tenor, and whenever one of them was away, my teacher asked me to fill in. I liked singing tenor in the boy's section. It made me feel masculine, and that was something that fulfilled me in a way I was still exploring.

I didn't think I was trans. It wasn't like I wanted to *be* a man. But I didn't want to be a woman, either. I had never been a girly girl, and I still didn't understand the fuss about makeup, high heels, fancy nails, and trying to look pretty. My regular outfit was a pair of jeans, a T-shirt, Vans, and my dad's wedding jacket that he'd let me borrow once and had never asked me to return. It was a dark-brown blazer that fit me to a T and made me feel sexy and cool. Not sexy in a girly way, either. Sexy in a strong way. When the weather warmed up, I switched to wearing a red plaid button-down, open, over my T-shirts. But then people thought I was a lesbian. Honestly, I got that social cues served a purpose, but it was infuriating that so many folks made instant assumptions about people based on what they were wearing.

Anyway, I'd rather be mistaken for a lesbian than a basic white girl any day.

I didn't consider myself a lesbian, though, because I was definitely attracted to guys, whether they were cis or not. There were a couple of transmen at my school that did it for me, too. But I'd had crushes on girls and had even enjoyed some fumbling explorations. Honestly, I didn't care what body parts people had. If I liked a person, and they were smart and appealed to me in a physical way, their gender wasn't important. So, did that make me bisexual, or was pansexual a better term?

And I was so horny, with no outlet that I wanted to consider at the moment. In a world where COVID was still circulating, it was almost impossible to think about kissing someone on the mouth. I supposed I'd want to eventually, but at the moment, it wasn't something I had to worry about.

The trouble was, I kind of wanted to worry about it.

02 Lending a Hand

MY THERAPIST worked in an office on Kilborn Avenue. According to their website, they still had power and were encouraging patients to keep their appointments if they could. I figured I might as well keep mine. There was nothing to do at home.

My mom dropped me off and drove to the nearby mall, which also had power, to get some shelf-stable grocery items.

"How are things, Dan?"

Fiza Faheem was in her thirties. She wore bright, cheerful head scarves to fulfill her religious and cultural obligations, and used carefully applied makeup to bring out the colour of her green eyes. She had a beautiful smile and the ability to cut right to the heart of a problem.

"Well, except for all the death and destruction around me, I'm okay, I guess."

Fiza frowned. "Is your home all right?"

"Oh, yeah, except, no power. Which kind of sucks."

"Sure."

"How about you?"

"Well, I've got the office, but I don't have power at home, either. I've been making coffee and toast in the kitchen here."

"Oh. That sucks." I mean, her office was pretty swank, but still.

She smiled and shrugged. "It is what it is. Did you try out any of those relaxation strategies I gave you last month?"

Was she seriously talking about relaxation strategies

after this wild storm had ripped through and taken out hundreds of hydro poles? What the hell was wrong with adults these days?

"Uh, well, after that storm? The strategies aren't helping much."

"Oh, I'm sorry. I suppose what happened a few days ago is giving a lot of people anxiety."

You think?

"Yeah. Probably." I shrugged, noticing a stain on my jeans.

Wonderful. I covered it with my hand in what I hoped was a subtle way.

"Where were you when the storm hit?" Fiza asked.

"At home."

She smiled. "Were you scared?"

"Not really. It didn't seem that bad, honestly. I was surprised to see all the destruction after. Except it's not surprising when you think about it. What with climate change and all that."

She sat back. "Do you think about climate change a lot, Dan?"

I stared at her for a long moment. "I guess. Define 'a lot.'"

She shrugged. "Every day? Every week?"

"Almost every day, if I'm being honest. Don't you?"

She didn't answer for a second. "I try to focus on things I can control."

"Like what?"

"Well, like my carbon footprint. Not owning a car. Stuff like that."

I nodded. "You don't own a car?"

"No. I take the bus or ride my bike."

"Cool." I mean, it was cool. And admirable. But . . . "So, you still think doing stuff like that is going to make a difference?"

"Maybe. I'd like to think so."

"I'd like to think so, too. But I'm not so sure."

We sat without speaking for a few moments. Maybe we were both thinking about the possibility of our world hurtling toward something that seemed pretty much unavoidable at this point. It was weird, but the act of discussing it with her actually did make me feel a bit better. Knowing that I wasn't the only one thinking we might be past the point of no return.

"Look, Dan, I can't tell you what's going to happen because I don't know. The future has always been unpredictable."

She looked serious now, and I paid attention. I was desperate for anything that might give me hope.

"All you can do are things within your power, which may not be much, but may be worth doing, anyway." She wrote something down on her pad of paper. "Are there any environmental groups at your high school?"

"Um, maybe. I don't really know."

"You could check that out. Doing something in line with the values they hold can give a person a sense of accomplishment and purpose. Whether your actions result in making a change or not, merely taking those steps can be worthwhile. And sometimes," she smiled, "you meet people who feel the same way you do. And that can be very helpful."

* * *

Attention Seniors: The Green Machine is organizing a clean-up of small branches and debris on school grounds. The damaged trees and larger objects have been cleared away by the City, but there is still lots to do. If you are interested in volunteering, these hours will count toward your volunteer requirement for graduation. Please meet us outside the front doors of the school at nine am tomorrow (Wednesday, May 25).

I stared at the email that had arrived through my school account on one of the rare instances my data provider had been working properly.

Hmm. Hadn't Fiza said I should become involved in something positive, even if it didn't affect real change? It would be cool to hang out with other people, even though the school wasn't open for actual classes. Plus, I was feeling restless after four days without power.

* * *

"You're actually going to school on a day you don't have to?" my brother said, raising an eyebrow.

"Not to do work, numb nuts. We're clearing debris."

"Sounds like fun. NOT."

"Whatever. Better than hanging out here with you."

* * *

Since the buses were detoured because of traffic lights that didn't have power, my dad offered to drive me.

"Do you have all your schoolwork under control? I know final assignments are coming due."

"Well, I can't work on anything right now, can I?" I said. "We don't have Wi-Fi."

My dad blinked. "Oh. True. I guess all your stuff is on Google."

"Yup."

"Well, I'm glad you've decided to help out with this. It's better than sitting in your room all day, moping."

"Yeah, sure, Dad," I said.

It was the same old, same old. 'Leave the house!' 'Get some exercise.' 'Go see a friend.''. How did he not understand that after two years of him and Mom and the freaking government telling us all to stay home, it wasn't like I could just flip a switch and suddenly want to be more social.

"Bye."

"See ya."

He drove off to his job and left me to my volunteering.

It wasn't quite nine yet, and there was only one other person outside the front doors of Ridgemont High School. I'd seen him around, and I knew he was in the grade above me. He had an uncommon name, but I couldn't remember it.

Of freaking course it's a Grade Twelve boy I don't know and who looks . . . incredibly attractive.

He wasn't much taller than me, I didn't think, but looked way cooler. He was all in black, with skinny jeans and cherry-coloured Docs. And he was wearing a *Greta Van Fleet* band shirt. Could he be more perfect? I mean, he probably wasn't president of the student council, which was a plus in my books, but he was probably a jerk. Nobody who looked that completely hot could be nice. That was simply the way of the Universe.

My palms started to sweat as I made my way forward, wondering if it had been a huge mistake to come.

03 *Levi*

THE GUY SMILED AT ME as I approached.

"Hi. Are you here to help with the clean-up?"

That smile. Man.

I nodded, hoping my voice wouldn't warble. "Yeah."

He held out his hand. "I'm Levi."

I grinned and took it, shaking it firmly.

"Dan. Short for Danielle, but we won't talk about that." My name sounded strange to my ears, and I wondered why I hadn't formally given it up. From what I'd heard, it was a simple process to change it on the school lists.

He tilted his head, examining me in a way that made my heartbeat increase but warmed me at the same time.

I smiled, running a hand through my short hair and pushing my bangs off my forehead. I really needed a haircut. It would still be considered short by feminine standards, but I liked it cut close and spiky all over. It was long enough now to be laying a bit too flat for my preference.

"What are your pronouns?"

I blinked. It was the first time someone besides a teacher had asked me.

"Um. She, her, I guess," I said, and then felt like that was wrong. But I was too tired to correct myself and what the hell did it matter, anyway? There were more important things to worry about than pronouns.

"You don't sound very sure," he said. "But that's okay. I'm still figuring mine out, too."

"Really?" He seemed so self-assured. "What are yours?"

"He, him. For now, anyway." He shrugged, then laughed. "I'm pretty fluid in most things. I'm not really in a rush to define myself."

He gazed around us at the empty parking lot.

"Geez, I hope a few more people show up," he said, frowning.

Really? Because I kind of like having you to myself.

"Yeah," I said, because it seemed to be the right thing.

His gaze returned to me. "I've seen you around. But you're not in grade twelve, are you?"

"Eleven. But I'm eighteen. My birthday's in December, and my mom wasn't in a rush to put me in school." I shrugged. It was a bone of contention. People tended to think I was a grade behind.

"Huh. That's interesting. I'm nineteen, for the same reason. What day in December?"

"Fifteenth," I said, already liking him. And we had one thing in common, at least.

"I'm on the twenty-first. Winter Solstice." He smiled again.

God, it lit up his face. I was already a goner. I hadn't expected to be romantically bowled over at a grounds-clearing meet-up.

"Cool," I said, acting like I wasn't imagining how it would feel to kiss him. His eyes were a deep grey, like skies on a cloudy day.

"Not a big talker, huh?" he said.

The look he gave me was kind, so I didn't take offence to that statement.

"No, I . . . I can talk."

Oh my God. Can I be any more ridiculous?

He puffed a laugh. Again, I didn't get the impression he was making fun. He seemed nervous, too.

"Well, I figured." He examined me like he was trying to figure things out. I was used to that from all kinds of people. But I wasn't used to the easy, affable way he had while doing it. The energy coming off of him was gentle and friendly.

"It's just . . . it's been a rough morning," I said.

He nodded. "I get you. Do you have power?"

For a second, I forgot about the outage and thought he was asking about something else.

"Oh. No. We've been out for days now."

"Me, too. So inconvenient." He sighed with dramatic emphasis.

I laughed. "Right? I mean, what the hell?"

Levi looked at the sky, where white, wispy clouds had gathered.

"Isn't it supposed to clear up and be sunny again today?" he said.

"Think so?"

God, we were talking about the weather. I started to hope some other people *would* show up, because I was so stressed out trying to think of something interesting to say, I was going to mess this up big time.

"I like your shirt," I blurted, making a vague gesture and clearing my throat. "It's a great band."

Now he grinned wide, and I felt my knees actually go weak.

Goddamn it.

"Josh Kiszka's voice!" he said, clutching a hand to his heart. "I think I'm in love with him."

I gulped as my heart sank. "I know, right? So beautiful."

That took some of the pressure off. And explained why I liked him so much. I was always falling for gay guys. I mean, seriously, how could you not? Gay guys are adorable and a lot less annoying than straights.

For some reason, knowing I probably didn't have a chance with him, made it easier to relax and just be friends.

"Do you live nearby?" I asked, scuffing the toe of my boot in the dirt. "I know this area got hit pretty bad."

"Yeah. My place is a few blocks away. That's why I'm here early. I've been so bored, y'know? Plus, this whole thing is my baby."

"Pardon?"

"I mean, I'm the one who's organizing this clean-up. I run the" — he made air quotes — "'Green Machine.' So, yeah, thanks for coming."

He looked around at the still-empty lot. "Hmm. Maybe you're the only one who got the email."

Right. The power outage.

"Oh, shit. That's true."

He laughed. "Oh well. At least you're here, Dan. We'll wait a bit longer and then get started. We can still make a difference."

"Sure," I said.

We waited, chatting about stupid shit, until twenty after. Nobody else showed up. I felt kind of bad for Levi, but he didn't seem upset.

"Come on. I've got plastic gloves and garbage bags in my car." Levi snorted. "Oh man, I sound like a serial killer."

"You're too hot to be a serial killer," I said, then felt my face heat. I hadn't meant for that to come out of my mouth.

Levi glanced at me and smiled. "Interesting."

Man, I was really starting to like this guy. I was in so much trouble. At least, maybe we could perv on hot guys together or something. That could be fun.

I tried to look on the bright side.

Levi's car was a beat-up monster that he seemed way too proud of. It was some kind of four-door sedan in a — I didn't even know what colour that was — kind of a puke green, slash shit brown.

"Wow," I said.

"It's all I can afford. My cousin let me have it for a buck."

"I think you overpaid," I said, examining the vehicle. Was it even road-worthy?

Levi laughed. "Probably."

He took out what we needed and handed me a pair of black gloves and a garbage bag.

"Seriously, Dan, thanks for coming. I would have been pissed and embarrassed if nobody had shown up."

"Well, you're welcome. I'm having fun, and we haven't even started."

"Yeah, me too. Go figure."

04 Contact Info

THE SKIES DID CLEAR.

And Levi and I made a difference. We picked up small bits of brush, shingles, and other various things that had been blown off roofs, garbage left over from the snow melt, and litter.

I had fun. It was a relief to be doing something, even though it might not affect anything more than the view of the school grounds. It still mattered, and I was glad I came.

Levi was funny and sweet — soft in a way I hadn't anticipated. His face betrayed every emotion he felt, and it was easy to read him. His scowl when he picked up a McDonald's carton that had been carelessly tossed onto the ground beside one of the bins, his delighted smile when we spotted a rabbit at the edge of the football field, and his calm diligence as we tied off the first of many bags of garbage. We spoke about random things at the beginning but, little by little, our conversation became more personal.

"Are you worried about finishing all your assignments?" I asked him. "This power outage couldn't have happened at a worse time."

Levi gave me a skeptical glance and shrugged. "At least it's not the middle of winter."

"Okay, well, true. Still." I sighed and scratched the back of my neck. "I kind of . . . procrastinated. And I was planning to catch up on everything this week."

"Oh crap. That sucks. The power should be back soon. And the teachers will be sympathetic."

"Hopefully."

"I've got most of my assignments under control, but not being able to work on them over the past few days will put me behind, too."

"Where are you going next year? Are you staying in Ottawa or going to school somewhere else?"

He blushed and looked at the ground, picking up a black shingle and shoving it into his bag. "I'm not going to school next year."

My head shot up.

He shrugged. "I'm gonna work and try to decide what my future will be."

Most of my friends were on the path to college or university after grade twelve, and I know my parents expected me to apply somewhere. I still wasn't sure, though, and it was refreshing to hear about other options.

"Do you work now?"

"Yeah. The family that fostered me owns a Greek restaurant. I work there part-time right now, and I'm going to go full-time once I graduate."

"Oh! That's really cool, actually." I meant his job,

of course. Then again, I'd never met anyone who'd been in foster care. All the stereotypes of foster kids didn't seem to match with Levi, but I guess that's why stereotypes were bad.

"It's all right. I don't mind it."

We'd put the bags of garbage into his trunk and now I was standing there awkwardly, wondering what to say.

"You should come by sometime. It's not far from here — at Conroy and St. Laurent. And, uh, here's my phone number if you want to make a reservation . . . or anything."

He took a card out of his pocket and wrote on one side of it.

"Here."

He handed it to me.

The business card had *Panagos Greek Eats* on one side in gold lettering, and Levi had scrawled his full name — Levi Fortin — and his number on the other.

What was happening here? I stared at the card, hoping I might figure it out.

He laughed again, and for the first time, he seemed nervous.

"I'm uh, not very good at this," he said, rubbing at his mouth.

"At what?" I forced myself to look up, once again blinded by his smile.

"Oh man. You seem . . . like a cool person. And I'm trying to . . . ask you out? I guess?" he shook his head. "Forget it, if you don't feel the same, I won't bother you."

"What? No, I like you, too. I'm just . . . not used to . . . being asked out."

He gave me a look. "Really? You're not making fun of me, are you?"

"No! What? I'm just kinda surprised that you would give me this."

He frowned, and I hastened to reassure him.

"But I'm so glad you did. I'll text you."

"Great." He nodded. "Good."

We stood there awkwardly for a moment. Levi looked at his car, but neither of us seemed to know how to make an exit.

"Oh shit, do you want a ride home?"

"No, that's my dad, there."

"Oh! Well, okay. Bye, Dan."

"Bye, Levi."

Levi's battered brown beast gave a sputter as he started it, but then hummed with a comforting steadiness as he waved and drove away.

My dad pulled up in our Santa Fe and stopped, keeping the SUV running. I opened the door and got into the passenger seat, still dizzy from realizing Levi had asked me out. Even though he was really hot, and I'd thought he was gay.

"Hi."

"Hi. Who was that guy?"

"Levi Fortin."

"Oh."

"His foster family owns Panagos Greek Eats," I said, still in a daze. I wasn't focusing as my dad pulled the car out of the school parking lot and we headed home.

"Well, how was it? Don't tell me it was only the two of you?"

"Well, actually . . . "

My dad's head flipped to follow where Levi's car had gone. "What? Really? I left you alone with a strange boy for the entire day?"

That broke my trance.

"Dad. Honestly."

"What? Do you know him? He looked awfully . . . mature."

"He's in grade twelve."

"Oh. Is he nice? I hope he was nice."

"He's really nice, Dad."

* * *

When we got home, the first thing I said was, "Is the power back on?".

My mom came out of the bathroom with one of the camping lanterns and a resigned expression on her face.

"Nope." She turned to my dad. "I'm getting tired of this, Frank."

"What am I supposed to do about it?"

"I don't know. But if it doesn't come back on by tomorrow, I'm going to be so upset." She turned to me. "Hi, Dan. How was the clean-up?"

"It was just her and a boy. A Grade Twelve boy. He looked suspicious."

I glared at my dad even though I knew he was kidding. "Why, because he was wearing black?"

"Maybe. Why would there be no other kids there? Maybe nobody likes him."

"Nice," I said. "I doubt that. He's awesome."

My dad did a double take at me, then said my mom's name. "Lorraine."

"What?"

"Dan's all aflutter over this boy."

"Dad! Stop. I'm not aflutter. What even is that?"

"Agitated. Interested. Confused."

"I'm not confused. I'm pretty sure he's gay."

"Oh." My dad smiled. "Perfect."

"I'm going to have a shower. Thank God the water heater works."

"I know, right?" my mom said. "That and the gas stove are the only things keeping me going."

As I turned to go up the stairs, I heard my dad talking to my mom.

"His foster family owns the Panagos restaurant."

"Really? Maybe we can get a discount."

I groaned and rolled my eyes, going into my room and shutting the door behind me.

05 Back on the Grid

THE POWER CAME BACK ON sometime in the night. I woke up to my clock flashing.

When I saw it, I closed my eyes again and sent a thank-you to the Universe. Then I pushed back my blankets and got out of bed.

"Power's back!" my mom said in a cheery voice as I went downstairs.

"I know."

"I'm making coffee."

"Hey, squirt," my dad said. "Hopefully your school has power so you can go tomorrow."

I raised my brows. "Now that I can get onto Google again, I don't even need to."

"Very funny," he said with a glare.

"Danielle, will you walk the dog, please?" Mom said. "I have a lot to do now that the power's back on so please don't disturb me too much."

"Sure. Okay." I grabbed a cup of coffee and put way too much creamer in it.

With our back fence still damaged from the storm, Izzy didn't have a yard he could use safely anymore. So, more dog walking. Luckily, Izzy had a pretty good track record for not shitting in the house.

"He'll need to go soon."

"I'm just having a cup of coffee. I'll take him when I'm done."

"Fine. Don't forget."

"I won't."

It was nice to get on Instagram and TikTok again. I'd gone into some withdrawal over the past few days.

I searched for Levi on Instagram and found him: @greenmachinelevi

His Instagram was full of artistic selfies, with his face half hidden, or only his shoulder showing, and the focus of the shot on what was in the background. I liked the aesthetic of it and laughed at several. He didn't have a problem making fun of himself.

My friend, Tara, texted me at nine-thirty.

Tara: power's on

Me: same thank god my service has been awful

Tara: yeah

Me: do u know anything about a levi at ridgemont

Me: grade 12?

Tara: levi fortin? he's cool i think

Me: yeah he asked me out

Tara: BRUH WHAT

Me: we did a clean-up at the school

Tara: i didn't hear about that

Tara: wait i just got it nvm

Me: yeah I don't think many people got it, literally only me and him

Tara: oh that sucks, are you going out with him?

Me: he wants me to call or text

Tara: why haven't you !!!

Me: its early

Tara: its 10 on a wednesday, everyones up. plus he probably puts dnd on like everyone else DO IT

I laughed.

Me: fine ttyl

Tara: ttyl DO IT

I sighed as I called up Levi's contact info. Was I really going to do this? Was I actually going to text him? What was I going to say?

I typed about six different messages and deleted them. Finally, I sent this one:

Me: hi levi its dan

Me: my powers on

While I was sitting there staring at my phone wondering how I could be so lame, I saw the three dots meaning he was typing something. Shit. I hadn't expected a response so soon. I mean, it made me happy, but I was starting to freak out. I wasn't used to romantic banter.

Levi: yay so glad

Levi: mine too

Levi: its a miracle

Levi: will u be at school tmrw

Me: if its open yeah

Levi: want to eat lunch w me?

Me: k

I sat there looking goofy and feeling weird for about ten minutes until my phone pinged again.

Tara: did u text him

Me: yeah

Tara: im calling u

I rolled my eyes and answered when my phone lit up with Tara's name.

"Dude!!!" she shrieked.

I had to hold the phone away from my ear. I put it on speaker but turned down the volume.

"Dan, Dan, Dan! What did he say? What did you say? Oh my God, this is amazing!"

"For God's sake, calm down. He's just a guy."

Tara made an incredulous sound. "A Grade Twelve

guy! A cute guy! A cute, Grade Twelve guy who likes you!"

"I guess." A weird, anxious feeling swirled in my belly. "Until I screw it up."

"What? How are you going to screw it up?"

"Tara, you know me. I'm not exactly what every boy dreams of. I'm *barely* a girl."

"Maybe he doesn't like girls!"

"Then I'm screwed, too!"

"No, no, no. What I mean is, maybe he likes girls who *want* to be boys."

I blinked.

"I don't want to be a boy. Not actually. But I don't see why I have to be a girl, either. Why are there only two choices?"

"I'm not trying to insult you. I think it's great. It's one of the many things I love about you."

"Well, you're one of the few."

"And so is Levi, apparently."

"Maybe."

"Definitely. And Dan, there aren't only two

NO LIMIT ON LOVE

choices. It's a spectrum."

"Sure, I know. Anyway, he wants to eat lunch with me at school tomorrow. If the school's even open," I said, trying not to sound hopeful.

"It'll be open," Tara said.

"How do you know?"

"Because my luck only goes so far."

06 Conversations on the Bus

I SPENT THE REST OF THE DAY practising my music solo and trying not to think of Levi Fortin. Of course, the song was romantic, so I inevitably did think of him.

I couldn't help remembering what Tara had said, about me being more masculine than feminine. She had a point, and I could forgive her for thinking I might be trans.

Honestly, I was okay with my body. Most of it. Luckily, I looked more like a boy than a girl. And the fact that I didn't wear makeup, do my nails, or wear dresses and skirts served to emphasize that fact. On good days, I imagined I looked like a cute boy. On bad days I imagined I looked like an ugly girl. Or at least, a weird one.

I'd come to accept the fact that straight high school boys didn't understand me. Only the gay and trans boys accepted me at face value and didn't expect the cultural cues of femininity that girls seemed obliged to adopt. They didn't seem to care what or who I was, as long as I was fun to be around.

I didn't like my full name, though, and I'd thought about changing it on the class lists. But it didn't seem worth the bother. I only had one more year at Ridgemont, and when I went to university, I could make sure to enroll as Dan. All my friends called me Dan. A lot of the time, my parents did, too. And boy, if someone made the mistake of calling me Dani on a good day, they got a glare and a cold shoulder. On a bad day, I told them I hated that nickname and to stop using it.

I was happy with who I was. I didn't think of myself as a girl or a boy. I was just Dan, whatever that meant. I wasn't happy that most of the guys I liked didn't get me.

* * *

On the bus heading to school the next day, the storm was the main topic of conversation. My mom was paranoid about bad weather, so we had gone down to the basement to humour her, since she'd seemed more freaked out than usual. She tracked storm damage on Twitter if severe weather was expected, and apparently, this one had been pretty bad going through Barrie and Toronto.

The lights at our place went out as soon as the wind hit, and my brother and I joked about a tornado, but we didn't believe anything really bad had happened. Sure, the rain and wind had been crazy, but the dog acted normal, so I wasn't worried. Weren't animals supposed to sense when there was danger?

When we came upstairs and noticed the fences down in ours and our neighbour's backyards, we could hardly believe it. And then my dad pointed to the tree on Jim's roof.

Jim was our neighbour out the back. Dad said Jim and his family had lived there longer than he and Mom owned our townhome. He was a nice guy, but he liked to work on construction projects early on Saturday and Sunday mornings, so I wasn't a huge fan. The two huge maples that were still standing looked like they'd been there for at least eighty years. Same with the one that was now lying on top of the house.

My mom pointed out that it had been wise to ride out this one in the basement.

Some of my friends didn't have any damage to their homes at all. But there was one guy, Kashif (his first name was Mohamed, but since there were so many Mohameds, he went by his last name at school), who had a tree fall on his roof. Kashif was as tall and as physically mature as a Grade Twelve kid when he'd started grade nine. He was very proud of the trimmed goatee he wore as a rebellion against his parents wanting him to grow a full one.

"Man, it was so wild," he said. "Baba and Mama were doing their afternoon prayers. Then we got the emergency alert, and they said we should all go downstairs. They took up their mats and finished in the basement while the storm went through. My sister and I figured we might as well join in, and I know I prayed the storm wouldn't bring our house down. I guess Allah listened since only a tree fell on us."

"True," I said.

Kashif swore he wasn't all that religious, but he pretended to be for his parents. On the other hand, maybe he pretended not to be to us, so we would think he was cool.

"There isn't a hole, but the roof will need to be repaired. Baba is pretty pissed about it."

"My dad was glad both his barbecues survived," I said. "And our glass table. It fell over with the umbrella in it and didn't even break."

"I was worried about my cat," Ahar said, putting on some lipstick and adjusting her hijab. "About five minutes after the rain stopped, she turned up, looking bedraggled. Poor thing."

Ahar had perfected the skill of applying lipstick in a moving vehicle. If I had tried it, I would have ended up looking like Bozo the Clown. Especially since I felt ridiculous whenever I tried to put lipstick on properly. I had only done it once and wiped it off with a tissue right after. I hated the stuff, and I hated the way I looked with it on.

Ahar had told me that her parents had given her the choice to wear the hijab or not. She'd said she had tried going without one when she was thirteen, but hadn't liked the way the boys had stared at her. She said the hijab was almost like an invisibility cloak, and besides, it was easier for her to just keep her hair in a bun and only worry about which colour hijab to wear.

"I'm glad your cat's okay."

"I think she's traumatized. She hasn't stepped out the door since the storm."

"Do you think we'll get more storms like that?" Kashif asked. "I've lived in Ottawa since I was four and I don't remember anything like it."

"God, I hope not. Or at least not for a long while,"
I said, thinking about climate change and wondering if
that was realistic.

07 Lunch Date

WHEN WE GOT OFF THE BUS outside the school, I recalled seeing Levi as he stood by the front doors, waiting patiently for people to show up for the yard clean-up. Spending the day alone with him had been great. Levi had told me his inbox was full of apologies from students who hadn't received the email and others who had had other obligations or no transportation. If fate hadn't thrown us together under such convenient circumstances, I still wouldn't know him and would never have had the nerve to approach him. I stayed in my lane at school, which was grade eleven.

Tara was waiting at my locker when I got there.

"Well, fancy meeting you here," she said with a grin.

"I tried to get out of it."

"I'm sure you did. Oh, except you have a date with Levi at lunch. You wouldn't want to miss *that.*"

"Shhh. Shut it."

"Why?"

"I don't want the whole student body to know about it."

Tara laughed. "Well, enjoy that for now. I think Levi's kinda popular. At least, among certain people."

"Really?" I said. "I was kind of hoping he was a loner like me."

"I think you're more popular than you realize. Most people like you."

"Do they?" I asked, with a sardonic lilt. Sure, I made friends easily. It was the maintenance thing that I had trouble with. I didn't bend over backward trying to please people. And I didn't go out of my way to hold on to friendships unless I really liked someone.

School was . . . normal. After we'd traded stories about the storm and the power outage, we got into the swing of a regular day. During my second-period Vocal Music class, my teacher called me over to speak to her.

"Dan, I'd like to practise your solo at lunch. Are you free?"

"Oh, sorry, I promised I'd eat lunch with someone."

Miss Jacobs raised her eyebrows. "Did you practise this week?"

"Yeah."

"Okay, can you stay *after* school?"

I sighed with relief that she wasn't insisting on a lunch-hour appointment. "Yeah. Sure."

She smiled. "All right. Can we practise again at lunch tomorrow, as well as after school today? You need to be comfortable with the piano accompaniment. And you'll be performing next week. Do you think you'll be ready?"

I frowned. "I hope so. I'm doing my best."

"That's all I can ask. You have a beautiful voice. You just need to practise."

I knew my voice was good. I sang in the shower often enough to understand that. But I hadn't ever tried to sing in front of a whole group of people. I'd already practised a couple of times with Miss Jacobs, and it *was* getting easier. She was so encouraging and kept reminding me to relax and project.

I started to get a little anxious as lunch time approached. It was silly. I had spent an entire day with Levi and it had been great. Why was I worried about spending forty minutes with him?

That was assuming he actually showed up where he was supposed to. What if he stood me up? What would I do then? How long were you supposed to wait around for someone before giving up on them?

But I ended up not having to worry about any of that, because Levi was standing by the doors to the auditorium when I got there. He was wearing red jeans and an oversized grey-and-black striped sweater that hung to his thighs like a medieval tunic, and white

Converse sneakers. He put a hand to his heart and closed his eyes.

"Oh, thank God. You didn't stand me up."

I couldn't help a laugh bursting from my throat. "Oh my God, I was worried about *you* not being here."

He opened his eyes and their calm grey colour made me happy.

"I'm a man of my word."

"Well, so am I."

Levi smiled and looked around. "Um . . . " he said.

"What?"

"Do you want to go to the cafeteria, or we could go outside?"

He was blushing in the sweetest way.

"Um, outside?"

He smiled and reached for my hand. When I didn't give it to him, he dropped his arm. "Okay, then."

I hadn't even processed the original action in time to respond to it, but it was too hard to explain that, so I just stood there while Levi gestured toward the main doors.

"I know this spot," he said. "Did you bring your lunch?"

"Yeah, it's in my bag." I gestured at the backpack I was carrying over one shoulder.

08 A Tasty Appetizer

"THIS IS MY SPOT," Levi said as he gestured to a large rock by the south side of the school near a copse of trees. "Well, not mine, exactly. But I like it."

"Wow. Trees still standing. I'm impressed."

I liked that Levi seemed a bit out of his depth, even though he was a year older than me, and honestly, way hotter. It made my own nerves settle down a bit.

He laughed. "Exactly. And somewhere to sit."

"Nice." I sat down and put my bag on the ground.

"What did you bring for lunch?"

Levi unzipped his burgundy satchel and pulled out a plastic container. "I try to grab leftovers from the restaurant if I can. Today I have dolmades and pita and a couple of pieces of souvlaki. It wasn't enough to make a sandwich."

"Dolma-what?"

"Dolmades. Dowl-*maa*-duhz."

"Dolmades."

"That's it. You?"

I unwrapped my sandwich from the tin foil. "PB and J. Boring but reasonably filling." I narrowed my eyes. "You're not allergic to peanuts, are you?"

"I'm not, no. But I don't like them."

"Oh."

He opened his container and used his long, slim fingers to dig a green cylindrical object from it. He held up what looked like a fat cigar made of leaves.

"This is dolmades. It's rice and herbs stuffed into grape leaves."

"Well . . . I'm not sure if that looks appealing to me."

"It's dope." He grinned and raised his eyebrows. "You want to try?"

I stared at his fingers, holding the dolmades carefully above his container, in case the condensation dripped. Both the food, and the idea of Levi feeding me, tempted me, but it was too soon after COVID for me to put my lips to someone else's meal. Or fingers. I didn't want to say that, so I tried to think of another excuse. While I was doing that, Levi noticed my hesitation.

"I know we've been conditioned not to share our food and drinks because of germs. I get it. You can have this one."

I wondered if he was actually this kind, or if he was putting on the dog a bit to make a good impression. But he oozed sincerity, so my doubts vanished in an instant.

"No, no. You eat it. I'm not sure I'd like it. I'm not a huge fan of . . . leaves." I listened to what I'd said and shook my head. "I'm a simple . . . girl." I frowned, because that didn't sound right.

Levi examined me for a long moment, but he

didn't say anything. He put the dolmades he'd offered me back in the container and stared at me with consideration.

"What?"

He scratched his chin. "I don't think you're simple at all. I've been trying to figure you out this whole time."

My cheeks heated. *Here I go again. Confusing people and being weird.*

"Sorry."

The disappointment that stabbed me in the gut came out of nowhere but felt very familiar.

"Dan, I didn't mean that in a bad way," he said, resting his palm on my knee. Then he jerked it back as if he'd done something he hadn't intended.

"Sorry. I'm sorry. I didn't mean to touch you like that." He seemed genuinely upset with himself.

"It's okay. It was my knee. And I'm wearing jeans. I don't consider it harassment."

"Some people might." He shook his head and chewed his lip. "God, I don't know how to navigate this without giving you the wrong idea. Or offending you. Or something."

"What's the right idea?"

He met my gaze and then looked away with a shy smile. When he came back to me, he said, "Well, I like you. And I'm trying to demonstrate that. But I don't know what your boundaries are." He licked his lips and continued, his kind eyes a much-needed ballast for my drifting thoughts. "I enjoy figuring you out. You're like this one-of-a-kind puzzle. You're fascinating."

I probably looked spaced-out and too caught off-guard to answer.

"I'm getting so much masculine energy from you, which I love. You're not — "

"I'm not like other girls? You know that's a meme, right?" I gave him a half-hearted and confused smile as I took a bite of my sandwich, so I'd have the excuse of chewing.

He sighed. "Look, I was dating this girl last year. And she was . . . I don't know . . . exactly what everyone thinks a girl should be. Which is bullshit of course, but humour me."

"Okay," I said, my mouth full of peanut butter and jam.

"She was so pretty, and she seemed really sweet at first. You know, kind and generous and said all the 'right' things."

"Sounds cool so far."

"Yeah. She's popular. And I was feeling . . . " he ran a hand through his hair. "I don't know, like I needed to prove I'm straight, which I'm not even a hundred percent sure of." He shook his head. "I told her that."

"What?"

"That I wasn't a hundred percent sure I was straight. She thought it was a joke, when it totally wasn't."

"Oh, God. Really? That's so…"

He shrugged. "I think . . . she took it as a challenge and she was all over me, like *all the time*. And if I couldn't keep up, she'd say these incredibly passive-aggressive things . . . like maybe I *wasn't* straight and she was just wasting her time, and if I wanted a boy to go get a boy."

"Wow. Damn."

"Yeah. But she was so sweet and kind to everyone

in public, it was hard for me to wrap my head around it. And I kind of thought maybe she had a point."

I started to shake my head, but he kept talking.

"Anyway, it didn't work out. And I've been spinning my wheels, trying to focus on school and getting good grades and not . . . not being lonely."

We gazed at each other, and I knew exactly what he meant by that.

"I had a really good time with you when you helped me clean up the school grounds. And I really, really like the fact that you don't seem out to impress people. That you're just who you are, and you aren't trying to be something you're not. You're so interesting and — " He laughed, and now he was blushing like a tomato. "I'm talking too much, aren't I? I'm going to eat my dolmades now."

I couldn't stop smiling. I put my sandwich down and held out my hand, palm up.

"I'd like to try one, please."

He was lifting one of the green leaf-wrapped things to his lips. He stopped and met my gaze again, raising his eyebrows — at my gall, I suppose. But then he smiled and placed the dolmades in my hand.

I held his gaze as I lifted it to my mouth and took a bite, then chewed carefully. I licked my lips before taking another bite and consuming the rest of the little appetizer with obvious hunger. It tasted good, a little different from what I'd expected, but I didn't care. I watched Levi's reaction, and it was . . . everything I'd hoped it would be.

If eyes could shoot flames, Levi's were setting me on fire. My actions had had the desired effect, and I was glad I hadn't screwed it up and turned this into some slapstick romantic comedy.

He cleared his throat and looked away, down at his own dolmades.

"Well . . . okay." He glanced up at me. "How was it?"

His voice sounded deep and rough, and his cheeks were flushed, but I didn't think he was embarrassed.

I inclined my chin. "Delicious. I've never tasted anything like it."

His mouth opened in astonished laughter as

he raised his brows. "Wow. If that's how you eat a dolmades . . ."

I pointed at him. "Stop right there. Don't make any assumptions."

"It's kind of hard not to."

Now I was laughing, and he was passing me another one, and this time I popped the whole thing in my mouth, because it was either go big or go home. And the look on his face was worth the risk of making a fool of myself.

"Dear God," he said.

My phone pinged and broke the moment. I glanced at it.

"Goddamn it. It's my mom." I read the text, which said:

There may be a storm this afternoon. Please be careful on your way home.

I rolled my eyes. "Oh, man."

"What is it?"

"My mom was paranoid about thunderstorms before the huge one. Now she's going to text me every time they call for possible showers."

I showed him my phone.

"Aww, that's sweet."

"I suppose."

I texted her that my vocal teacher wanted me to stay late and then asked if she could pick me up at four thirty because the buses came a half hour apart and I had to switch at South Keys.

She told me to text my dad because she wasn't driving in the rain.

"Oh, man," I said again.

"Now what?"

"I need to stay late to practise my music assignment, but she doesn't like to drive in the rain, so I'm supposed to ask Dad to pick me up. But he'll be making supper . . ."

Levi nodded, his forehead creased in thought.

Then he said, "I can drive you home. I've got my car."

"But you'd have to stay late."

He shrugged. "I've got some assignments I can work on in the library."

"Holy shit. You do like me."

"I do like you."

I shook my head.

"What?"

"You're the first guy who hasn't stared at me with a slightly disgusted expression on his face wondering what the hell I am, since I'm so obviously not a typical high-school girl. Maybe I'm not a girl at all."

I had avoided his gaze during that whole speech, and when I had the guts to look at him again, he didn't seem fazed.

"I don't care how you identify, Dan, or don't identify. You don't have to put yourself in a tidy little box for me. You shouldn't have to do that for anyone." He pushed himself off the rock and dusted off his jeans. "I'd love to drive you home today if it's okay. Even though I think that's the most heteronormative thing I've ever said to a . . . person."

I was a little stunned. "Okay. Yeah. It's fine."

"Awesome. We should probably get to our afternoon classes."

"Yeah."

"Of course, I'm only going to be thinking about you eating my dolmades."

"Pffftt!" I blew air and spit out between my lips, covering my mouth just in time, as I tried not to faceplant in the grass.

09 A Stolen Moment in the Dark

"OKAY, OPEN YOUR THROAT, DANIELLE. Use your diaphragm to breathe."

"Miss Jacobs, can you please call me Dan? That's my preferred name."

Miss Jacobs blinked. But then smiled. "Of course. I'm so sorry."

"It's okay. I'll try to relax and . . . open my throat this time."

An image of Levi's dolmades flashed in my brain,

and I had to force myself to focus and not laugh.

"All right, let's start over," Miss Jacobs said, her fingers hovering over the piano keys.

We went through the song three or four times, and I think I did get better. My voice warmed up, and I started to enjoy myself.

"Much better," Miss Jacobs said. "Your tone is so rich, Dan."

She glanced at the open door to the music room.

"You've got groupies."

My head spun around, and I gaped at the two students standing there. One of them gave me a thumbs-up before they turned and continued down the hall.

"Oh God. Now I'm nervous again."

Miss Jacobs regarded me with sympathy. "It might be beneficial to do some relaxation exercises before you sing. I can email you some links."

"Thanks."

A boom of thunder sounded, and we looked at the ceiling, then at each other.

"I guess storms are going to be a bit nerve-wracking for a while," Miss Jacobs said. "After that last one."

I smiled and tamped down the spike of nerves that had hit. It was only a storm. A plain old, regular storm. And I knew that because my mom had not texted me anything to let me know it might be severe.

"Yeah."

"But there's no reason to think we'll get another one like that for a while."

"Uh," I said. "Climate change? Maybe not this one, but there could be a storm like it over the summer." Or worse, I thought.

"Well, I hope not," Miss Jacobs said. "Raising twins is hard enough. Without Wi-Fi, it's horrendous."

I laughed and so did she. When I got to my locker, I texted Levi.

Me: done.

Levi: great finishing up my essay so cm to the library.

Me: ok

As I walked through the halls, my footsteps echoing through the empty space, I glanced out the windows at the driving rain and wind, hoping the sudden storm would let up soon. I didn't particularly want to go out in it. On the plus side, the fact that I hadn't gotten a text from Mom or an Emergency Alert boded pretty well.

When I opened the door to the library, Mr. Coombs glanced up from the checkout desk and gave me a wave, then pointed toward the study carrels that were tucked into the back corner. I don't know how he knew I was looking for Levi, but I smiled and nodded, and followed his silent directions.

I guess it was because Levi was the only one there. He was hunched over his laptop with his AirPods in, concentrating on his work, with his phone face up on the desk in front of him and his back to the room.

I stopped about a foot from him and pulled up his contact info, then hit FaceTime.

His phone lit up and he glanced over, then thumbed the accept button. As his face showed up on my phone, I let out a soft laugh and whispered, "I'm behind you."

Levi turned and saw me, pleasure evident on his

face. "Well played."

I shrugged. "I didn't want to scare you."

I closed the FaceTime app, and Levi did as well.

"Are you ready — " I said, just as the lights went out. "Oh, damn."

"Shit."

A flash of lightning lit the room for an instant, as the sound of the sheeting rain and rising wind intensified. The sweeping beam of a flashlight found us a moment later as Mr. Coomb came toward us.

"Don't worry. There are batteries in the EXIT signs."

He nodded toward the black space behind him, and sure enough, the EXIT sign at the entrance glowed red. But that was the only light other than Coomb's flashlight.

My phone pinged, and I glanced down to see a text from my mom.

Mom: Power's out again!

"Wonderful," I groaned.

"What?" Levi asked.

"Power's out at my place. That was my mom."

"Is she hiding in the basement?" Levi's voice held a playful tone, and I appreciated it. I wasn't exactly scared. But after what had happened a week ago, I was definitely on edge.

I thumbed my phone and waited for a response, then looked at Levi. I could only see the outline of his face, but I smelled peaches or clementines — something citrusy that I thought was coming from him.

Or was that Mr. Coombs?

A text came in. I showed it to Levi.

Mom: Not yet. I may end up there. It's a coping mechanism.

Levi smiled, and Mr. Coombs stepped away. "I'm going to check the hall. Are you all right here?"

"Sure," Levi said.

"Yeah," I agreed.

Levi glanced at the door to the library as Mr. Coomb's went out, and it swung closed with a click.

"This could be the start of a horror movie," he said.

But my mind was going in a different direction. It had to be Levi who smelled so good because Mr.

Coombs had gone.

"Or a romance," I said. *What the hell?* "Wait, sorry, not a romance, we just met, and I think — "

"Kiss me," Levi said.

Our audible breathing sounded intense in the darkness as another flash of lightning lit him up, and I stretched out my hand and rested my trembling fingers on Levi's jaw, which was prickled with light stubble.

"Where's your mouth?"

Levi puffed a minty laugh and helped me find it. Our lips came together as thunder boomed.

My pulse went wild. Something rose up in me, and I had to tamp it back as I tried to be polite and not go for it like a crazed animal. But the lightning was inside me, and the thunder was my heartbeat as I clutched Levi's arms and tried not to fall over.

Levi gasped and pulled back, panting. He wiped a shaky hand across his lips.

"Holy hell," he whispered.

"Sorry. I'm sorry," I said, all of a sudden worried that I'd been too much, that I'd held the kiss too long.

"For what? That was — I mean, wow."

"Yeah," I said, "Wow."

He smiled and ducked his head. "My lips are tingling.

"So are mine."

We laughed.

"You know, you — " he shook his head. "Never mind."

"What?"

"You kiss like a boy."

I felt myself light up inside, like that was what I'd only ever wanted to hear.

"Really? Wait, you've kissed boys?"

"One or two. Nothing more. Not yet, anyway."

"Not . . . yet. Okay. So, you're bisexual?"

"I guess. Or . . . I'm probably pansexual."

"What's the difference?"

He leaned against the wall, and even in the semi-darkness, I saw his gaze drift over me, and he licked his lips.

"Well, I don't care about gender, you know? It's

irrelevant to me." He shrugged and moved back toward me. "There's a whole rainbow out there."

He pushed a bit of hair off my forehead as all the breath left me and he leaned forward, as if to kiss me again.

And the lights came on.

Levi stepped back as Mr. Coombs came back into the library, followed by two students.

"Hallelujah!" Mr. Coombs said. "That wasn't too bad. Not like the last time."

It was hardly raining at all now, and the sun was trying to come out.

Levi and I exchanged a regretful glance.

"Guess you should drive me home," I said, trying not to smile as everything inside me thrilled at the memory of that kiss and the things that it might portend.

"Yeah, I guess so," Levi said, subtly adjusting himself before he strode past me toward the door. "Taxi's leaving."

10 *Advice*

WE ARGUED OVER RADIO STATIONS.

"But Chez one-oh-six is what my *dad* listens to! You like *classic* rock?" I said, my chin dropping because life wasn't fair.

Levi side-eyed me. "It *is* my car. But you are my guest, so which station would you prefer?"

I thought about it, trying to imagine what would make me sound coolest. Or maybe I should just be honest.

"Well, I like eighty-eight point five. Usually."

He snorted.

"What?"

"So basic."

"Oh, shut up," I said, as we burst out laughing. "So, I'm basic. Big deal."

"You, Dan Carlisle, are so *not* basic. Your taste in music, on the other hand . . . "

But he changed the station. And *Greta Van Fleet's* "Heat Above" was playing.

I pointed at the display with my eyebrows raised and gave him a cheeky, silent smile.

"Okay, that's not so bad," he admitted.

"Not so — that's *Greta Van Fleet*, my man. There is no way they are uncool and you know it. Josh Kiszka, remember?"

"Oh, I remember." Levi closed his eyes as if he was picturing the famous musician and sighed.

I smiled.

"I have *great* taste in music."

I felt comfortable in Levi's car with him, and sure of

myself. He grinned and tapped his fingers on the steering wheel as he drove down the road toward my house.

"This is it here," I said. "Five eighty."

"Ooh. The storm did hit you guys pretty good," he said, as we drove past sawed-up tree branches piled at the side of the parking lot entrance.

"You should see our backyard fence. Or the place where the fence *should* be." As I said it, I realized I should probably invite him in for a . . . what? A snack? A coffee? Did he even drink coffee? I so did not know how to do any of this.

"I can get out here," I said, gesturing to the curb. "My house is that one, with the red mailbox. My mom is in a fight with the condo board because we're only supposed to have black mailboxes or some shit."

I rolled my eyes and put my hand on the door handle as Levi chuckled.

"Your mom sounds amazing."

"She's something, all right. Did you . . ." I swallowed thickly " . . . want to come in for a second?"

"No, I have to get home. And it looked like it

killed you to ask me that."

"Only because of my family! You're so cool and they're . . . well, they're . . . an acquired taste."

Levi's face lit up with his widest smile. "You think I'm cool?"

"All right, all right," I said, pushing the passenger door open and stepping out. "Don't let it go to your head."

"Oh, Dan. *Dude.* It already has. See ya."

"See ya," I said, grinning as I shut the door and gave him a wave.

I bounced up the path as he turned his car around and drove away.

He'd called me *dude*, and it hadn't made me want to punch him. I was such a goner.

* * *

I managed to avoid any probing questions from my folks about how I got home, so nobody new I'd been with Levi. I didn't want to keep him a secret, exactly, but I didn't want to answer any questions along the lines of "Is he your boyfriend?" because, honestly, I had no idea. It seemed a little too soon to say, and I didn't know how these things worked.

In fact, boyfriend or not, I didn't see him again until the following week because he was finishing up some assignments that he'd put off and now were due. He really wanted to graduate, even if he wasn't going to university anytime soon.

So, I concentrated on my own schoolwork and hung around with Tara and Jules and the gang. Tara and Jules were a couple, so I asked them how you were supposed to know when you were dating someone or just friends.

"Dan. Seriously?" Jules said.

"What?"

"You should be talking about this kind of thing from the get-go. It's important to have clear expectations," Jules said, adjusting her glasses.

"Exactly," Tara concurred, taking Jules's hand and twining their fingers.

We were sitting on the stone wall beside the

school's entrance. Nobody seemed to notice Jules and Tara holding hands, because there were all kinds of relationships at Ridgemont, and nobody gave a damn about it unless there was drama going on. Then people paid attention.

And Tara and Jules were the least interesting couple at the school. They'd met up at the beginning of grade nine, and by Christmas, they were together and had been ever since.

"But it's barely 'got-gone.' We only started hanging out last week."

"Still," Tara said, glancing at Jules for support. "It's important to know where he stands on sex and relationships."

I squinted my eyes and grimaced.

"Is it, though?" I really didn't want to have that conversation with Levi. Not yet.

"Well, don't wait too long," Tara said. "You should definitely get that all sorted out before you guys kiss or anything."

My sudden discomfort must have been obvious

because Tara covered her mouth and shrieked, causing some heads to turn.

"He kissed you!"

"Oh my God, shut up!"

"Sorry. But *he kissed you*?" she stage-whispered.

I looked at the ground as heat filled my cheeks. "Actually . . . "

Tara grabbed my arm. "Dan?"

"Technically, I kissed him." I shrugged. "We were kind of in the library. When the power went out. It just happened."

Tara was bug-eyed. "Oh my God. Who are you and what have you done with Dan? You dog, you!"

"Do you need condoms?" Jules asked.

"What? No! What?" I said.

Tara's head snapped around. "Why do you have condoms, Jules?"

"Because I never used them. They hand them out at Pride, remember? I've got a drawer full."

Tara calmed down. "Oh. Right. Jules has condoms if — "

"I don't — "

"Sorry, for *when* you need them."

"I can buy my own condoms," I said. Were we really having this conversation?

"But these are free," Jules protested. "Except, you better check the expiry date."

Tara's face scrunched up. "Do condoms expire?"

"Duh," Jules said, rolling her eyes.

"What do you mean, 'duh.' Like, do they leak acid or something?"

Jules laughed hysterically as I gazed around to see how much attention they were attracting.

"No, but expired condoms won't keep the babies away," I said, in an aggressive whisper. "I'll get my own, and I don't think I'm anywhere near needing them just yet."

In the back of my mind, I wondered if I should get some, for whenever I decided I *was* ready. My mom had always told me to be in charge of my own protection when it came to sex, and I intended to do that. I'd been on the Pill since I was fourteen, to control my acne and manage my menstrual cramps, but the Pill didn't protect you from other stuff.

Anyway, I was not getting into this with them. Levi and I had only shared one kiss — *almost* two — and I didn't even know if we were dating, or just friends, or what. But maybe it was time to figure that out.

As it turned out, Levi solved the problem for me.

11 Trolls

Levi: r we dating or what

He dropped this question into the middle of a stupid text conversation about *The Mandalorian*. We had been debating the ethics of Grogu eating that fish woman's eggs, but when I saw this, it took me a second to change gears.

Me: depends.

Levi: ???

Me: r we going on a date

Levi: do u want to?

Me: hmm

Me: sure

Levi: saturday?

Me: sure where and when

Levi: i'll pick u up at 2 it's a surprise

Me: bruh

Levi: see ya

I walked into music class with a smile.

"Dan, can I talk to you?" My teacher took me aside.

"You're scheduled to perform in class on Monday. Will you be ready?"

Would I?

"Hope to be."

"Do you have time to practise at lunch tomorrow?"

"Sure."

"Perfect. You're going to do so well, Dan. I can feel it."

"Thanks."

I wished I felt as confident as she sounded.

I saw three possible outcomes. One of them was

me simply standing there, not being able to sing a single note. Another involved me singing but tanking. And, of course, there was another outcome that had me acing it, impressing everyone, and earning top marks.

The actual result of all my preparation and anxiety was kind of a crapshoot at this point. At least practice went well.

"Dan, I think you're ready!" she said after the final run through. "That made chills go down my spine."

"Really?"

"Good chills. Not the scary kind."

I smiled. "You really think that was okay?"

Miss Jacobs put a hand on my arm.

"Dan, I think you're going to blow their minds. Now, look. If I were you, I'd put this aside until Sunday, then sing it through on your own a few times. On Monday, if you can get out of your first class early, you can come here, and I'll warm you up a bit. But that's it. We're not going to perform it again until class on Monday. And you will be great!"

I gave her a doubtful look.

"If you say so."

"I do. You've worked hard on this. Don't think that won't reflect on your mark, regardless of how you perform at the assessment. But I know you're going to rock it."

"Thanks, Miss Jacobs. It's been fun practising."

"Try to keep having fun when you perform it."

"Okay."

I kind of wished I could keep meeting Miss Jacobs in the music room and practising different songs and other styles. But the day of reckoning was coming. And I still had the rest of this week to get through, plus my date with Levi on Saturday.

Life seemed just a bit overwhelming.

* * *

The next day at school, Tara had a meltdown by her locker. Jules was with her but didn't seem to be giving her much sympathy.

"But I don't have time!" Tara wailed.

"Why did you wait so long to start all these projects?" Jules asked, hands on her hips, and a long-suffering look on her pixie-like face.

They spoke at the same time:

"I don't know! I always do this!"

"You always do this!"

Then they broke out laughing, which cut some of the tension. But Tara still looked upset.

"You have to prioritize," I said, "Which one is due first?"

"Um, English. I need to get it in tomorrow."

"And how much is done?"

"Maybe half?"

"So, finish that today, before you go to bed. Look it over in the morning, and hand it in. What's next?"

"Digital Arts. It needs to be in by Sunday."

"Okay. You can do it, Tara. You do this every year."

"She does this every year," Jules confirmed. "And she usually makes it. But there's always this moment, this exact one, when she realizes the next five days will be hell because she has to work non-stop. Whereas I prefer to space my assignments out, so I can do a little bit at a time."

"Yeah," I said. "I keep planning to do that, too. Never works out."

I had to go to my homeroom class, but I gave Tara an encouraging look and a thumbs up. She gave me a weak smile, then buried her face in Jules's shoulder. I knew she'd be okay, but I didn't envy either of them.

I finished my final written assignment last night because I didn't want anything except my vocal performance hanging over my head this weekend. And since Miss Jacobs had insisted I not practise much, I would be able to enjoy my date with Levi, whatever we ended up doing.

He wouldn't give me any hints, except to tell me to wear jeans and boots. Maybe we were going to play paintball? Or laser tag. But you could play laser tag in shorts and a tank top. Actually, didn't they give you coveralls for paintball?

I couldn't figure it out.

I was walking to my locker, which was in a different bay, when I heard Levi's name. I stopped and turned and saw three girls huddled together by the locker bay. They were looking right at me and talking in whispers. When they saw me looking, they turned and giggled even harder.

Then one of them turned, looked me up and down, shrugged, and said, in a stage whisper:

"She looks like a boy. No wonder he likes her."

My cheeks flushed as a surge of anger rose inside me. But now they were walking away, and it wasn't worth confronting them. The words didn't bother me. It was the tone of voice that she had used, and the disdainful way they had looked at me.

I took a deep breath and continued on to my first-period English class, trying to forget about it. I didn't want to waste another thought on them.

But as I approached my locker after English, on the way to my next class, I noticed the same three girls again. Since I'd never seen them in this part of the locker bay before, I figured they were deliberately stalking me. Like the last time, they pretended to ignore me. But soon, I heard Levi's name, and one of the girls glanced up at me, then looked away.

Whatever. I ignored them, which was my most-used strategy for dealing with this sort of thing. If people didn't get a rise out of you, they got bored and moved on to someone else. So, I got my stuff for my next class and shut my locker door.

When I got to my locker before lunch, there was a piece of paper stuck to it.

DEADSHIT. All caps.

Which was more amusing than anything, because wasn't that an insult from 2018? Still, it made me mad. I was sure those girls had put it there, but how could I prove anything?

I ripped the paper off my locker, crumpled it and tossed it as far down the hall as I could manage. I didn't like to litter, but it wasn't my garbage in the first place.

There were no more incidents that day. Which was a relief, because I had many more important things on my mind.

I didn't tell Levi about it. He didn't need to worry about that, on top of trying to finish his assignments.

We'd been texting off and on through the week, but I hadn't seen him much. We had plans for Saturday, though, and I was excited.

An actual date. With a guy I liked. With my . . . boyfriend? Could I call Levi my boyfriend? Maybe after Saturday, if everything went well.

* * *

Tara was so mad the next day when I mentioned the note on my locker.

"It's no big deal," I said. "Pretty cringe, if you ask me. Do people even use that word anymore?"

"If I were you, if I saw them pulling the same bullshit, I'd walk right up to them and ask what their problem is," Jules murmured.

"Yeah, like that's not going to cause more problems than it's worth."

"Or maybe then they'll respect you and leave you alone," she said, biting a piece of her carrot and shrugging.

"There's only two and a half weeks of school left.

I'm not getting pulled into some sort of Mean Girls vortex."

Jules giggled and Tara nodded.

"I feel that," Tara said, holding up her fist.

We bumped and got down to eating.

"Do you have any idea where Levi's taking you on Saturday?" Tara asked when we'd finished and were chilling in the middle of the cafeteria. Most of the others had gone outside.

I shook my head. "Nope. I'm not sure if I like the suspense or if I'd rather know what I was in for."

"I think it's romantic," Jules said, with a smile. "He's obviously putting a lot of thought into it."

"Well, I guess we won't know that until we find out what he's got planned. What if it's something boring?" Tara said.

I raised my eyebrow. "It's not gonna be boring. Levi could never do anything boring."

Jules flashed a grin to Tara. "I think someone's in love."

My cheeks heated. "I'm not — we've only been

talking since last week!"

"And *kissing*."

"Oh my God." I rolled my eyes, but I couldn't help smiling, remembering that awesome kiss in the darkened library.

"Is he a good kisser?" Jules asked.

"Best I've ever had," I said with a smile. I still didn't know quite what had possessed me to simply go ahead and plant one on Levi's lips in the library, except that he had a nice mouth, had smelled amazing, and he had asked me to.

I could always blame the storm.

12 Mindy

THE NEXT MORNING, I got a text from Levi asking if he could call me.

I texted back that he could, and in a moment, my cell ringtone went off.

"Hey," I said, after swiping the call.

"Good morning."

"To what do I owe this pleasure?"

He laughed, which was good, because he probably wasn't about to break up with me or cancel our date.

"Hey, has Mindy been bothering you?"

"Huh. I don't know who that is."

"Oh, of course, sorry. She's my ex. She's being an asshole."

"Good thing you guys broke up, I guess."

"Seriously." He sighed. "I'm starting to hate her now."

"How come?"

"Darrick said she and her posse are trailing you around and talking shit."

"Oh? I hadn't noticed."

"I can't tell if you're being sarcastic . . . "

"A little. It's no big deal. They're annoying, that's all."

"I'm sorry, though."

"Not your fault. But maybe she's still into you."

"I wish she wasn't. We really . . . were not a good match."

I waited a second longer than I meant to. "Do you think we're a good match?"

"Don't you?"

"Yeah."

"I'll see you on Saturday. Bye."

"Bye."

I put my phone down and noticed that my heart was thumping like an unbalanced dryer. This was all happening so fast, which was totally better than not happening at all.

* * *

There was a bigger note on my locker when I got there, with *BOYFRIEND STEALER* written in the same black Sharpie.

I was so over this whole thing. I looked around to see if those girls were anywhere nearby. I didn't see them, but a kid who was in my chemistry class was leaning against the lockers, watching me. I think his name was Bradley.

"It was Mindy Lowry and her squad." He rolled his eyes and put his phone away. "I saw them tape it up there. I was going to take it down, but you got here right after they left."

I grabbed the note off my locker.

"Which way?"

He pointed down the hall. "Toward the cafeteria."

I nodded and went in that direction.

The three girls I'd seen yesterday were walking together down the hall, laughing and talking. I heard my name and Levi's, and the word *bitch*.

"Mindy," I said with some force. Sometimes you had to call a person's bluff, and I was pissed off enough to do it, regardless of the consequences.

Mindy Lowry was as basic as they came. In fact, I was disappointed in Levi for having dated her. But I supposed a boy could be led astray by her artfully applied makeup and engineered selfies. I wasn't scared of her or her two flunkies.

She turned at the sound of her name, and when she saw me, her default smile faltered. So far, all of her bullying had been stealth attacks, so I had a feeling she wasn't looking for a direct conflict.

Even so, she had found one.

"Yes?"

"I think you forgot this," I said, lifting the paper that had been taped to my locker so that she could read it. "I'd appreciate it if you didn't leave your shit on my shit anymore."

Her friends stopped walking and watched for a reaction.

Mindy looked at the paper, then at me, and gave me an even sweeter smile. "I think you have me confused with someone else."

"No, she doesn't. She knows exactly who you are, Mindy."

My head swivelled to Levi, who had somehow materialized beside me. He was shooting a furious look at his ex-girlfriend.

Turned out that Levi looked even hotter when he was justifiably angry at someone.

He held out his hand for the piece of paper, and I gave it to him. Then he crumpled it up and held it out to Mindy.

"Here. Take it. We don't want it."

She started to speak. "It's not — "

"Take it, Mindy. And don't bother us anymore. Or we'll take this to the principal. And also Bradley's cellphone video of you and your crew defacing Dan's locker."

Mindy scoffed, but I could see the unease under the surface.

"He doesn't have a video."

Levi shrugged. "Are you sure about that? He was there when you did it."

"Her name's Danielle, you know," Mindy said, eyeing me with distaste.

"Still better than 'Mindy.' But I prefer to go by Dan," I said.

Levi threw me a quick smile, then waved the crumpled paper at his ex-girlfriend.

"Take this. Or Brad and I are going to see Mr. Kumar."

She stared at the crumpled paper, her cheeks flaming red. I couldn't tell if it was anger or embarrassment.

Maybe a bit of both?

Her friends had abandoned her. She licked her lips. Then her hand shot out as she snatched the crumpled paper from Levi.

"Whatever," she said, as she turned and made her way down the hall.

"Bye, Felicia," Levi said under his breath.

"Wow, that was . . . " I put a hand to my forehead " . . . impressive."

"I can't believe I dated her."

"I'm struggling to wrap my head around it."

Levi turned toward me, apology in his eyes.

"I'm sorry you had to deal with that."

"A piece of paper taped to my locker? I think I'll be okay."

Levi reached out for me, and I took his hand. He laced our fingers.

"I saw you call her out." He swallowed. "You're hot when you're mad."

"Hmm. So are you. But you didn't have to take over. I would have been all right."

Levi nodded, bringing our laced fingers to his lips. He gazed at me as he kissed my knuckles.

"I was worried for Mindy."

13 Coming Out

I SLEPT LATER than usual on Saturday and woke to the smell of coffee and pancakes. When I came downstairs, Jake and my mom were at the table, arguing. I'd heard their raised voices, but the coffee was calling me.

"Jakob. You're on your computer all day."

"So?"

"It's not good for your eyes."

"Tell that to the school board. All my schoolwork is digital."

"That's true," I said as I passed them.

"Stay out of this, please." My mom was half watching the news and half ragging on my brother about his screen time.

The smarmy announcer in his conservative outfit delivered the following line with his standard, bordering on cheerful expression: "Climate scientists say we are heading toward a worst-case scenario, and it's up to governments to slow down emissions, something that very few are doing effectively."

"Awesome," I muttered and went into the kitchen. "So glad to have a future to look forward to."

Mom rolled her eyes. "Don't catastrophize."

I stopped dead and exchanged a sober look with my brother.

"It *is* a catastrophe. Maybe you all should have been taking it seriously twenty years ago," I said. "Then maybe we'd have a chance."

I went into the kitchen, not wanting to get into this with my parents, who didn't seem to understand how dire the outlook for the next fifty years looked to my generation.

Dad was at the stove, cooking bacon and eggs. He wasn't a big fan of pancakes.

"Good morning," he said, glancing at me.

"Morning," I said. "Smells good."

I grabbed a mug and poured myself some coffee, then added two sugars and a bit of milk. I went to sit at the table with my mom and my brother.

"Mom. Wow. I just had my eyes checked, remember? They're fine," Jake insisted.

"I still think you need to find something else to do on the weekends. Besides computers and video games."

"But — oh my God. What do you want me to do?"

"Go outside! Take a walk. Breathe some fresh air. Take this goddamn dog for a walk."

"Mom!" I said, shocked at her reference to our beloved Izzy.

"Sorry. I'm sorry. I barely slept last night. Your dad was snoring."

"So were you," came from the kitchen.

"Pancake?" my mom asked, nodding toward the

pile of flapjacks on the plate in the centre of the table.

"I'll get one in a minute," I said, taking a sip of my coffee. One thing I could say about my parents, they made good coffee. "Can I talk to you about something?"

Jake side-eyed me as he chewed his pancake. "Oh boy."

I narrowed my eyes at him.

"Sure," Mom said.

"Yeah, I — this is kind of awkward, but I feel like — I think, I want you guys to use a different pronoun for me."

My cheeks heated. I gazed at my coffee as I waited for a response.

"Not you, too," Jake said.

I glared at him. "What do you mean?"

He rolled his eyes and opened his mouth to say more. But didn't.

"No, really, what do you mean?" I insisted. I'd had enough coffee now to deal with his bullshit.

"I don't know. Seems like nobody wants to just

stick with the classics. Girls are she, boys are he. It's pretty simple."

"No, it isn't." My mom said it before I did. I looked at her, and she shrugged, then continued. "It really isn't as simple as that, Jake."

"Whatever."

I cleared my throat, just as my dad came in with a plate of bacon and a bowl of scrambled eggs that he placed on the table.

"I'd like you to use 'they, them' for me. It just makes me . . . more comfortable. I don't know."

"Fine," Jake said, and stuffed another piece of pancake in his mouth.

My mom's smile wobbled. "I'll try?"

"What's this?" my dad asked as he took his seat and lifted his mug of coffee to his lips.

"I'm just . . . I'm asking you guys to use they/them when you refer to me, instead of she/her, which makes me uncomfortable."

My dad made a choking noise and almost spilled his coffee. He set it down on the table and picked up a napkin to wipe his lips. "Do you really think that's necessary? We already call you Dan most of the time."

"Dad. I wouldn't be asking if I didn't think so."

"Are you . . ." My dad looked me up and down. "I mean, you're not going to actually . . ."

He didn't really know the terminology, and I gave him points for not using the wrong words, but simply waiting for me to understand what he was asking.

"Not at this time, no. I don't think I'm trans."

"Oh."

"You don't have to look so relieved," I said.

"I'm sorry. It's just a lot to take in."

"What is? The fact that I want you to use they/them?"

"Dan, honey, we didn't have these kinds of ideas when we were younger. We didn't use they/them in the way they do now."

"You just used it."

"Oh shit," she said. She had the grace to laugh. "I guess I did."

"I don't see what the big deal is," Jake said. "If

Dan really wants us to use they/them, then I think we should."

My parents swivelled their heads to stare at Jake, who froze with a piece of pancake halfway to his mouth.

"What?"

My parents looked at each other, and my mom smiled while my dad rolled his eyes.

"We'll do our best," my mom said. "But I'm not making any guarantees. I can barely keep your names straight these days."

"Yeah, speaking of which, I really don't want Danielle used at all for me anymore."

My mom threw her hands up in the air in frustration. "But what do I use if I'm really, really mad at you? That isn't in the parent handbook. I'm supposed to call you by your full given name. That's the rules, Dan."

She was kidding, and I smiled. "I guess you'll have to think of something. Or just, never get mad at me."

Jake snorted. "Yeah, good try."

I could see that my mom had questions, but she

refrained from asking me anything in front of my dad and my brother. After we'd eaten breakfast and I'd gone upstairs to decide what to wear for my date with Levi, there was a knock on my door.

"Can I come in?" my mom asked.

"Sure."

She twisted the knob and opened my door, coming in and closing it behind her. She smiled and sat down on my bed.

"You know, I love that you're comfortable enough to ask us to change your pronouns. I'm glad we've created an environment where you feel supported to be yourself, Dan."

I nodded. She stayed silent, and I knew she was waiting for me to say more.

"I'm still figuring things out, you know? Because I've never felt like a ... typical girl. Or a girl at all, really."

My mom nodded. "You never went in for the frilly pink dresses I tried to put you in a few times."

We laughed.

"True."

"You were always more of a rough and tumble, overalls kind of kid. But girls can be like that."

"I know. That's just it. I don't think I want to be a boy. I'm not trans. Or, at least, I'm not trans right now. But I'm not comfortable being a girl either. I don't even like the *idea* of gender." I gazed at my mom. "It seems like a ridiculous concept to me. Why can't people be who they are and ignore the expectations that seem tied to whether you're male or female?"

My mom's forehead creased like she was thinking that over.

"You know it's okay to not define yourself. You can just be you, without a label."

"Yeah, I know. But I'm starting to feel like certain labels fit me, and I want to try using them."

"Okay."

"Like, there's a nonbinary gender identity, and I kind of feel like that's . . . me. Because I don't believe in the gender binary. Like, at all."

"So, that means you don't feel like a boy *or* a girl?

Or is that gender fluid? God, this conversation makes me feel old."

I laughed. She was good at cutting the tension in a conversation.

"So, yeah, I think nonbinary is what I like best, but I'm still kind of working it out. I want to use Dan as my name exclusively. You and Dad and Jake usually call me that, anyway, so it's not much of a problem. And I'm not saying I hate the name Danielle . . . I know you chose it for me, but it just . . . doesn't suit me anymore?"

My mom smiled, and I think she was fighting some strong emotion. Her eyes looked shiny.

"Look, your dad and I chose names for you and your brother because we needed something to call you when you were young, and you couldn't choose for yourselves. We picked out names for our *babies*. Both you and Jake have grown so much, and you're still in the process of becoming. You get to decide who you want to be. Not us."

I swallowed, feeling a rush of emotion myself.

"Yeah."

"We will always support you in doing that. We might have advice or things we'd want you to be aware of before you make any big decisions, but we will be on this journey with you until we're not around anymore."

"Wow, way to get morbid."

She laughed. "You know what I mean."

"Thanks, Mom."

She smiled and stood up. "If you ever want to talk about this more, my door is always open. Well, until nine-thirty, when I go to bed."

I nodded. "Um, this seems like a good time to tell you that someone's coming to pick me up at noon."

Her face lit up. "What? *Who*?"

I laughed.

"It's the guy I met at the school grounds clean-up."

"Well," she said, pleased as punch that I'd confided in her. "He sounds like a king. Isn't that what you kids say about people who are slaying at life?"

"Oh God, Mom. Stop."

"Wait a second. Is he the Grade Twelve boy Dad told me about?"

"Uh. Yeah."

"Well, you better get ready! Where are you going on this date?"

"Your guess is as good as mine."

14 Surprise

AT ABOUT 11:50, Levi texted me.

Levi: im here

Me: ok one sec

I grabbed my wallet and shoved it in the back pocket of my jeans, then took the stairs two at a time as I went down.

"Hold on, squirt." My dad looked up from his iPad. "What time will you be home?"

"I . . . I'm not sure."

He peered over the rims of his glasses. "Where are you going with this young — person?"

Oh shit.

"I don't know."

"Hmm."

"I'll text when I find out." I narrowed my eyes. "I know you and Mom track my location. I'll be fine."

He stared at me for a moment, then puffed a bit of air out between his pursed lips.

"I'd feel better if I could meet this kid."

I stared at him, and he stared at me. It was a battle of wills that I always lost.

"Okay. Fine."

I texted Levi.

Me: can u come in

Me: my dad wants to meet u

Levi: omg ok

My dad smiled and winked.

"Thank you. And just so you know, if you were my son and a strange Grade Twelve boy was going to take you somewhere, I'd be just as concerned.

I rolled my eyes.

"You don't have to be. Levi is great."

"That's good. I'd still like to meet him."

My mom was gardening out back. I felt some relief that she wouldn't be here, but then the slider opened, and she came inside. The dog, who was leashed to the foot of the sofa so he didn't run out the door when it opened, got excited to see her and started barking.

"Dad texted me. We get to meet Levi?" my mom said.

"Oh my God," I groaned.

"Hey, we get to have some fun," my mom said.

The doorbell rang. The dog went wild.

My mom took off her gardening gloves and stood there in her rubber boots. At least she had a bra on and a T-shirt with no holes. I should be thankful.

I took a deep breath and went through the dog gate, shutting it behind me. I opened the front door, then blinked several times.

"Quiet!" my mom told the dog.

"Izzy, enough!" my dad shouted.

"Sorry about that," I apologized for the noise.

"Hey," Levi said, with a broad smile, ignoring the chaos and bravely standing his ground.

"Uh." I scanned him from head to foot. "Howdy?"

He was wearing skinny jeans and an untucked flannel button-down — blue — with the sleeves rolled up, and a cowboy hat. He doffed the hat and showed it to me.

"You like it?"

"I could be persuaded."

"It's a hint," he stage-whispered.

My gaze roamed over him again. I mean, he could pull it off.

"Are we going to a hoe down?"

He didn't reply, but laughed as he stepped into the house. His cheeks flamed red, and I wasn't sure if he was embarrassed to have to meet my parents, nervous about seeing me again, or worried about showing up in Western gear.

"Mom. Dad. This is Levi Fortin. Levi, these are my parents. Kill me now."

My dad waved from his spot on the sofa, and my mom gushed.

"Hello! We just wanted to meet you before you took our daught — I mean, our child — out for the afternoon," Mom said.

"Sure. No problem, Mrs. Carlisle," Levi said politely.

"Where exactly are you going?" my dad asked.

Levi looked at me for assistance. I knew he didn't want to tell me, but there was nothing I could do about my dad's request.

I shrugged.

He returned his gaze to my dad.

"Um, it's kind of a surprise, Mr. Carlisle, but if you give me your number, I'll text it to you right now."

"Six one three, four eight nine, seven seven two five."

Levi thumbed his phone. In a second my dad's phone pinged. He glanced at the text, a slow smile spreading on his face as he nodded sagely.

"Excellent." He looked up and smiled at Levi, then at me. "Have a great time."

"I certainly hope we will, sir. I'll have Dan back by six."

I rolled my eyes as I laced up my Docs while cursing under my breath.

"What is this, the fifties?"

"Nice to meet you, Levi!" my mom said, with a glint in her eyes.

If she said one word later about how cute she thought Levi was, I would probably throw up in my mouth. Even though it was true. I glanced at his ass in his skinny jeans as he turned to open the door.

"Okay, man. You've gotta tell me where we're going," I said, as I slid into the passenger seat. "This is killing me."

"You seem okay to me. I like that shirt."

"Thanks. Although it's not quite as — " I looked him over " — uh, down-on-the-farm, as yours."

Levi grinned. "Well, hold onto your hat, because it's a sign of where we're headed."

We drove south outside of the city limits. I glanced at him and raised an eyebrow.

"You're not driving me to a secluded spot to murder me, are you?"

He laughed. "You watch too much TV."

"Actually, I don't. I'm obsessed with true crime YouTube videos."

"Ah. Well, no, no plans to murder you."

"Cool, cool."

"Not yet, anyway." He grinned.

I rolled my eyes but fought a smile. I pressed the button to lower my window and looked at the scenery as the wind ruffled my slightly too long hair.

"Geeze, the tree damage is bad out here," I said.

"The Northern Tornadoes Project says there was a major downburst right through here that was five kilometres across and thirty-six kilometres long." He waved around us to where downed and broken trees wound through upright forest in a chaotic pattern.

"The what-now?"

He glanced at me. "They're a group of scientists from Western University who analyze damage from severe storms and have the authority to make an official report. You know, decide whether it was a tornado or, as in our case, a derecho." He frowned. "Group might be overstating it. It's actually two guys." He shrugged.

"I've never heard of a der — a dera —" I tried to pronounce the unfamiliar word.

"Dare-eytch-oh. It's Spanish for 'straight ahead,' because the winds of a derecho go in one general direction, unlike the spiralled winds of a tornado."

"Hmm. Seems like the damage is about the same."

"Actually, what we had is worse than a tornado, because it's more widespread. But because nobody's ever heard the word before, I don't think the wider public really gets what went down here. The word tornado has more of an impact on people's understanding." He shook his head. "It's as if there were multiple tornadoes in different places across the city."

"Shit."

"Yeah."

"Are we going to be cleaning up debris again?"

"If I said yes, would you be mad?"

"No. I had fun doing it with you at the school."

"Same. But, no, we aren't."

"Okay."

"I called the place we're going, to ask about storm damage. They said they weren't hit too badly, and it's been cleared and dealt with."

I opened the weather app on my phone. I generally used it for a temperature reference, but I found myself checking it more often these days. There was a Thunderstorm Watch in place.

"Uh . . . are we going to be outside?" I asked, staring at my phone.

"Yeah. For part of it."

My text notification pinged, and a message came in from my mom.

Mom: FYI thunderstorm watch for our area. Keep an eye on the weather!

I texted OK back and turned to Levi.

"What's wrong?" he asked.

"There's a thunderstorm watch. My mom just texted me, and I saw it in my weather app."

"Oh shit. Well, we'll be inside for a bit. Then we

can assess and see how things look."

"Okay."

I still had no idea where we were headed, until Levi slowed the car and took a turn off the highway, and signs for *The Circle J Ranch* began to appear.

"Uh . . . " I said, my heart beginning to beat frantically. "Is that where we're going?" I sat up straighter and looked at his profile, my heart beating faster. "Are we going *horseback riding*?"

15 Mucking Stalls

"WE CAN RIDE if you're up for it and the weather cooperates. Or we can just hang out with the horses."

Excitement rose inside me, followed by the unexpected fear of being caught out in the woods in the middle of a wild storm. God, was I going to turn into my mom? I shuddered at the thought.

"I want to go for ride! Obviously!"

I pushed away the fear and told myself that if the skies looked bad before we rode out, we could let the bad weather pass by and then go. I hated that I even had to think about it.

He laughed. "Yeah, your brother said as much."

"What? What has Jake got to do with this?"

"I found him at school and asked if you knew how to ride. He said you used to ride all the time, but hadn't had the chance to go in a while."

I tried not to bounce in my seat as Levi drove along the dirt road.

"I haven't done it in so long. Is that really what we're doing today?"

I may have never gone from wary to totally pumped in so short a time, ever.

"We do have to muck out a couple of stalls first but then, yeah, we can ride."

I nodded and I'm pretty sure I had a goofy smile on my face.

"I've been volunteering at the Circle J since I was nine. I used to take lessons and now I just ride when I can. It's Western riding, not English, by the way. My preference. Not so formal. I just want to ride, not get into show jumping or dressage."

"That's so awesome. God, you hear so many stories about kids in foster care, but I guess for you it wasn't that bad," I said, and then realized that just because he got horseback lessons out of the deal didn't mean it hadn't been hard in other ways. "Shit, I'm sorry. I don't know anything about it. That was a stupid thing to say."

Levi's expression seemed complicated, but he reached out and covered my hand, squeezing it, then letting go. "It's okay. I'll tell you about all of it sometime. But not today. Anyway, you're right. I totally lucked out with my foster parents, which is rare. A lot of kids aren't so lucky."

Levi turned the car onto a dirt track that led us over a hill and onto the grounds of an expansive ranch.

"Levi," I said as I gazed at the white farmhouse and horse barn and the corral full of horses and forgot all about the storm watch. The blue sky stretched out above us, dotted here and there by feathery white clouds. "This is . . . I can't believe you picked horses!"

"There's more to me than dolmades, you know."

I laughed.

He parked the car, and we got out. I resisted the urge to run over to the fence and start petting horses, in the interest of appearing cool.

"Why don't you go over and introduce yourself," Levi said, nodding toward the corral where a group of haltered horses milled about. "I'm going to let Carrie know we're here."

"Okay," I said, glad to be able to indulge my instincts while Levi headed toward the farmhouse.

The powerful smell of horses, straw and manure filled my nostrils as I approached the grey fence. A large bay nickered to me and shoved its nose over the top rung of the fence.

"Hello, lovely," I said, petting the velvety skin around the horse's nostrils as it snuffled and snorted.

A smaller grey horse sauntered over and shoved the other aside in order to greet me.

"Well, hello."

I fished my phone out of my pocket and took a picture of them, then posted it to my Instagram story.

That would intrigue my friends, especially since I hadn't taken the time to put any text over the photo. I put my phone away and concentrated on petting soft horse faces until I saw Levi striding over.

"Getting acquainted?" he asked, clicking his tongue.

The horses lifted their head and moved toward him.

"Yeah. They're so pretty!"

"This one's Echo," Levi said, scratching the grey horse's wide muzzle. "And the bay is Cricket. The paint over there is Whisper."

I must have looked starry-eyed. Levi laughed.

"I can tell I chose the right thing to do on our first date."

"Oh my god. You absolutely did."

"Well, if you can handle hard labour for an hour, we can choose two of these horses and ride out."

I glanced at the sky, then at Levi.

"You mean, on our own?"

"Sure. I know the trails, and we'll take Echo and Whisper. They're great."

"I've never gone with just one other person." Oh, but I so wanted to!

"Come on. We've got stalls to clean."

As we walked past the farmhouse, I noticed a group of young people eating lunch at some picnic tables, and a group of saddled horses hitched to a fence near the gate to a huge open field.

"Those are the camp kids. They pay for the day and have a trail ride in the morning, eat a packed lunch, then go out again with Jen in the afternoon."

"Wow. That's cool. I would have loved to have done that when I was a kid."

"I mean, you still are a kid."

I narrowed my eyes at him.

"I'm eighteen. Legally an adult."

Levi simply smiled and led me into the barn and over to a wheelbarrow parked beside an empty stall. He grabbed a shovel from its holder and handed it to me.

"I know you're not afraid to get your hands dirty."

"This is a lot more fun than picking up garbage." I

took a deep breath and let it out. "Don't you just love the smell — "

"Of horse shit?"

" — of horse shit."

We laughed, and Levi handed me a pair of leather gloves.

"Get to work, cowboy."

We shovelled horse shit and soiled hay into the wheelbarrow, then carted it to the compost pile. Then we got fresh straw from the loft and spread it over the stall floor with a long rake. It was the most fun I'd ever had with a guy. But it was hard, sweaty work, and by the time we'd cleaned four stalls, Levi told me we were done.

"We can keep working. I don't mind," I said, wiping moisture from my brow with the back of my arm. I felt energized and focused, and I liked knowing that my hard work was going to make four horses comfortable.

Levi arched a brow. "Don't you want to go riding?"

"Oh shit, yeah. Yes, I do."

"All right. There's still a storm watch, but there

doesn't seem to be anything on the radar as of yet."

"Great. That makes me feel better."

Knowing Levi was keeping an eye on things and not thinking I was ridiculous for being nervous made me feel better about it.

We cleaned up, and Levi took me to the tack room. He grabbed two riding helmets off the wall and passed one to me.

"Safety first."

I put a hand to my chest in mock astonishment. "But, my hair!"

"Very funny."

I grinned and put it on, fastening the buckle under my chin, while Levi did the same.

Levi grabbed a lead rope and handed me one.

"Hey," I said.

"Yeah?"

"Is there a polite way for me to say how amazing your ass looks in those jeans?"

Levi laughed. "Don't worry about being polite. It's overrated. And, uh, thanks. I'm glad I wore them."

We walked back to the corral, and Levi lifted the latch of the gate. As we entered their space, the horses moved toward us, their eyes bright with interest and curiosity.

A feeling of lightness and anticipation that I hadn't experienced in a very long time filled my chest.

Levi captured the paint gelding by the halter.

"Here, you take Whisper," Levi said. "He's real gentle and responsive. And a bit lazy, so he won't run away on you."

I nodded, attaching the clasp of the lead to the ring on Whisper's halter, excitement swirling in my belly.

"He's so pretty!"

"Oh, he knows it. Look at him."

Whisper tossed his head and nickered as if he agreed with Levi's statement. I laughed.

"Echo likes to play coy sometimes," he said, making his way over to the grey mare. "But I brought a secret weapon."

He pulled a carrot from his pocket and enticed the mare over, shooing the other horses who expressed a similar interest. Whisper, who also wanted a bite of juicy carrot, rolled his big eyes at me and pulled against my hold.

"Sorry, buddy."

"Here," Levi said, breaking the carrot and passing me a piece as he fed Echo the other half and clipped the rope to her halter.

"Thanks."

I gave Whisper the bit of carrot, and he seemed appeased. He was more than happy to follow me out of the corral and into the barn, with Levi and Echo leading the way.

16 *Living in the Moment*

IT TURNED OUT THAT GROOMING HORSES was like riding a bike — once you learned the technique you never forgot it. It helped to have Levi beside me if I needed reminding, but I remembered how to gently pick up the horse's hoof and how to use the hoof pick. I recalled how to carry a saddle and its blanket, how to buckle the girth, and which side of the horse I should be on when I did all of this.

"You do know your way around horses," Levi said,

and his approval made me a bit giddy in a way that was a little embarrassing and a lot of fun.

"Yeah."

"How come you stopped riding?"

I shrugged. "I don't know. I started high school, and it seemed like I didn't have the time anymore," I said. "Although I'm starting to regret it now. I forgot how much fun it was."

We led Whisper and Echo out of the barn.

Whisper seemed really large all of a sudden, and Echo only slightly smaller. If you were going to ride a horse, you might as well ride a big one. Levi swung himself up onto Echo and smiled at me. "You okay?"

"Sure. I got this," I said, placing the toe of my Doc Marten boot in the stirrup. I looped the reins over my left arm and grabbed the pommel of the saddle, then put my other hand on the back of it and swung myself up. That one action was like a muscle memory, and my head flooded with memories, helped by the creak of leather, the jingle of metal, and the vibrations as Whisper's skin quivered beneath me and he shifted his feet.

"Wow," I said. "Everything looks so good from up here."

"Yep," Levi said, bringing Echo around to face me and Whisper. "Your stirrups okay?"

"Hold on." I spent a minute adjusting them, then nodded to Levi. "All right."

"Cool. Let's go."

He urged Echo toward the gate that divided the homestead from the fields.

"I've really missed this," I said, aware of Whisper's strength and the rock of his gait as we followed Levi and Echo. His ears flipped back-and-forth as he moved toward the field with a palpable eagerness, and I chirped to him and praised him.

"Better than any antidepressant," Levi said. "I try to come every week, but that doesn't always happen."

"That's awesome." I didn't comment on the antidepressant remark. Tara had been on one for a year or so, and it had been a game-changer for her. But I could see that getting regular exercise and doing something fun on the regular could benefit a person a great deal.

"It helps me keep my sanity."

"Ha-ha. Your what-now?" I joked.

He laughed. "Funny."

I sighed, listening to the sound of Whisper's hoofs thudding in the dirt and the creak of the latch as Levi lifted it and pushed the iron gate out of the way. He was leaning forward, half out of his saddle, and, yeah, his ass looked freaking amazing in those skinny jeans.

"View is great from back here," I said.

He glanced behind him and caught my blatant ogle. The smile that spread across his face made my heart sing.

"It's not too bad from here, either."

He held my gaze as he guided Echo through the gate, then waited at the side for me and Whisper to pass through.

* * *

The trail Levi took led through mostly intact forest. There were only a few areas where downed trees were cordoned off from the main trail. Whisper and Echo plodded through the undergrowth as the songs of blackbirds and cardinals rang out. We caught glimpses of wildlife, but our ears picked up more of the nature surrounding us. It was like a tonic to my nerves after everything that had occurred recently. The sun pierced the trees with its dappled light, and even the mosquitoes had decided to give us a break. I completely forgot about the storm watch. I'd even silenced my phone because I figured we'd be aware if any bad weather was heading our way and I didn't want to be disturbed as I enjoyed my first ride in years.

As we emerged from a thick stand of trees, the view opened up over a stretch of sparkling blue-green water and I gasped.

"Oh, wow," I said. "It's so pretty."

"Yeah. This is my favourite spot."

I was hot and gritty from the dust and dirt, and boy, that water looked fresh and inviting.

"Can we go in?" I said.

"With the horses? Sure. They'd probably love to

cool off," Levi said. "Here, follow me."

I guided Whisper behind Levi and Echo, as he led us into the shallow water at the edge of the stream. A gentle current played along like water fairies danced there. The horses nickered to each other as they splashed through it, and Levi and I smiled.

"You hungry?" Levi asked when we brought the horses back to dry land.

"I could eat a horse," I joked. "Oh, sorry, Whisper. Not you."

"Good thing I brought sandwiches," Levi said, swinging down from Echo's back.

We sat on the grassy bank of the stream and ate the sandwiches Levi had brought. I'd noticed more cloud cover coming in but nothing that looked too bad. I was having so much fun I almost didn't care about the weather. Levi had said the radar looked clear, so I wasn't going to let the prospect of an isolated shower ruin my day.

We chatted and watched the tethered horses chomp grass in the shade. They were handsome animals.

Whisper had huge splotches of dark brown here and there over a white background. He had a wide one over his right shoulder and the side of his neck. The other part of his neck was white. Another spread of brown started behind his left ear and covered most of his face, but for his right cheek and the underside of his long muzzle.

I supposed paints were named for the fact that they looked like the product of a DIY project gone wrong. But the random contrasting colours made each one a unique piece of art.

Then again, Echo, with her dappled grey coat was equally gorgeous.

Levi lifted his cola.

"A toast to our first official date."

I smiled and clinked my can with his.

We sat there for a few moments in silence.

"I'm glad you were the only one who showed up for the clean-up."

"Me, too."

Levi blushed and looked down. "I'd kind of given

up on dating, to be honest. And then, you came along."

"I'm glad you took another chance."

"Me, too."

"I guess, in a way, that damn storm had something positive come out of it."

I gave him a look. "I mean, true. I didn't think of that."

"I don't mean to minimize it. Every time I read about the forest fires, or the flooding in other countries, I get this horrible feeling in my gut. I try not to think about it a lot of the time because things do look bleak right now, what with the climate, and the war in Ukraine, and all the political upheaval in the U.S."

"Yeah."

"But I guess we can't control any of that. All we can do is appreciate what we have right now." He gestured to the horses and the stream. "We get to ride these gorgeous horses and be together, right now. I think," Levi said, his forehead creasing, "I think we need to enjoy these moments even more, because who knows what the world will look like in forty or fifty years."

His words hit me deeply.

Levi was right. We had to hold on to these moments and appreciate the things we had, rather than waste them with worry about an unforeseeable future. If climate change, by some miracle, didn't end up killing us all, then I'd have wasted my life worrying that it would. And if the worst *did* happen, I'd have wasted all those precious years not savouring every single thing that was at stake.

17 Shelter from the Storm

"I NEED TO GET WET," I said, peeling off my jeans with the casualness of a cowboy needing a dip. "You coming?"

Levi stared at me for a second, his gaze taking in my lower half in the black cotton boy-shorts as I unbuttoned my shirt and tossed it aside.

"Yeah. Okay," he said, and followed more slowly. "Wait up."

"*Catch* up," I said, sticking my tongue out at him and striding into the shallow water. I was electrified and on fire, feeling free and uninhibited for maybe the first time in my life. The horses, the hot guy beside me shucking his clothes, the beckoning, sparkling water — it was like a drug, and I was so, so high on it all.

The water felt deliciously cool on my sweaty skin as I sank into it. Then cold drops splashed me in a sudden assault, and I gasped. Levi, in just his boxer briefs, stood in water up to his ankles with a mischievous look on his face as he bent to splash me again.

"Stop," I laughed, moving into deeper water. The stream was shallow all the way across, so we had some room to play. "Asshole!"

He did stop, which gave me the reprieve I needed, and I ran over and grabbed his wrist, tugging him into the stream.

"Oh shit!" He almost slipped but grabbed onto my waist to steady himself. We stared at each other, our hair dripping from the splashing, our chests rising and falling with our hurried breaths.

"God," he said. "You look . . . "

I raised my chin, curious as to what he would say.

"What?"

"You look . . . wild. And free."

I grinned and splayed my hand over his chest, where he had a spread of light hair and light-brown nipples that were pebbled from the cold of the stream. Now his fingers wrapped around my wrist, and he circled his other arm around my back, pulling me against him.

As we found each other the outside world faded away. I lost myself in the kiss, feeling things with Levi I'd only ever felt on my own before.

It wasn't until the thunder crashed that we realized it was raining.

We pulled apart and stared at the grey, overcast sky, which had been clear moments ago. Or perhaps we'd been standing here in the stream longer than I'd thought.

"Shit," I said, then looked at Levi, panic rising inside me where there had been desire a moment before.

The rain seemed to get harder by the second. It streamed down Levi's face and chest as he stood in the thigh-deep water in his soaked boxer briefs. I wasn't so terrified that I didn't appreciate the sight for the space of a half-second.

I ran for the bank, checking that the horses were where we'd left them. They were shuffling their feet and pulling at their leads that we'd hitched to a tree branch.

"We need to get away from here," Levi shouted over the noise of the rain and the thunder.

"But where do we go?" I said, as I tugged my shirt over my head and pulled on my jeans, then shoved my bare feet into my Docs, not bothering to lace them. Levi got dressed as well, and we moved toward the horses.

"There's a better spot over there!" He pointed toward the middle of a group of small trees surrounded by bigger ones.

"But we're not supposed to go under trees!"

"We're in a forest! We're also not supposed to be in the water or in the middle of a field."

The sudden storm raged around us as Levi untied

the horses and mounted Echo.

"Get on Whisper and follow me," he said. "Trust me."

I was so scared I could barely function. Panic gripped me. What if this storm was another derecho? What if the winds and the rain got stronger? There was no protection out here.

I forced myself to get onto the horse and not urge him into a gallop in the direction of the barn, because that would mean crossing open fields.

I followed Levi, because I did trust him.

When we got under the smaller copse of trees, he slid off of Echo and helped me down from Whisper. He must have felt me shaking. He took my face in his hands and made me meet his gaze.

"Dan. It's going to be all right. I promise."

I nodded, even though I didn't believe him. Another boom of thunder and flash of lightning made me jerk with fear.

"Hey." He smiled, and I focused on the calm in his eyes. "The horses can tell you're freaking out, and we really don't want them to panic. Can you get it together?"

Okay, okay. The horses. I need to stay calm for the horses.

I nodded. "Okay. Yeah."

"Cool."

He kissed me again, and his rain-wet lips on mine managed to convey the sense of calm and control I needed.

When we broke apart, he told me to tie Whisper to the tree beside us, next to where he attached Echo. We huddled beside them, Levi cradling me in his arms while I buried my face in his neck.

After a few more moments that seemed longer than they probably were, the rain lightened up and the thunder faded. Levi's secure hold on me never let up. He kept me close and safe beside the shuffling horses until the birds started singing again and the sun broke through the trees. I felt its heat on my cheek before I could manage to open my eyes.

It took some time for my pulse to get back to normal. And then I was mortified.

I wriggled free of Levi's embrace.

"Oh my God. I'm so sorry," I said, feeling my cheeks heat and reliving all of the humiliating fear and panic, and buzzing with adrenalin that I didn't know what to do with.

"For what? For being scared?"

I shook my head. "For acting like a kid."

I glared at the sky, which looked blue and innocent again. But I was pissed.

Levi kicked at the wet grass as I stood there with my arms crossed protectively over my chest.

"So, you got scared. So, did I."

"No, you didn't."

"Oh yeah? Give me your hand." He reached out for it.

I gazed at him with suspicion before slowly extending it. With gentle fingers, he took it and placed it over his heart, which I could feel beating like crazy in his chest.

My eyes widened, and the anger inside me faded. He'd been freaked out, too. He just hid it better.

"I think everyone in this city is going to be terrified of storms for a while. Maybe for a long time. What happened here a couple of weeks ago was intense. People died. Not many, considering. But they did."

I nodded, finally feeling my pulse start to even out as Levi's steadied as well. He held my hand securely to his chest, and that anchored me and helped me to calm down.

"Yeah."

He smiled, and it was almost as good as seeing the sun come out.

"I was shitting my pants," he said. "Well, not literally. But then I got worried I might *literally* shit myself, and you would never want to talk to me again."

I puffed a short laugh, and it felt good to relax.

"That ... probably wouldn't be a deal breaker for me," I mused.

He raised his eyebrows, calling me out.

"Okay, well. I'd like to think I'm better than to stop dating someone for an involuntary bowel incident." I glanced at the sky. "In a situation like this."

He rolled his eyes and let go of my hand. I let it drop.

"Okay, then. Let's get these horses back to the stable."

We had to go back to the stream to grab our helmets and Levi's backpack.

On our way back to the stables, we passed the group of giggling day camp kids headed out for their afternoon ride. They'd been smart enough to stay at the ranch until the storm had passed.

"I guess you got caught in that?" the trail leader asked with a sympathetic smile.

At least they assumed we were drenched from the rain and not from goofing around half-naked in the stream.

Levi pushed his damp bangs up under his helmet and grinned. "It didn't last long."

"Sure. You should have seen all these kids high-tail it into the barn at the first sign of rain. And when that thunder hit, I had to calm them down."

I felt better about my own panic. Levi was right.

We would all be paranoid about severe weather after that storm.

"I bet," Levi said. "Anyway, have a great ride."

He looked at the sky, which had cleared and brightened completely. The rainwater glistened on the grass as the only reminder of the bad weather.

18 Taking a Chance

THERE WERE FOUR TEXTS from my mom when I checked my phone:

Mom: FYI, there might be a storm!

Mom: Dan? Are you inside?

Mom: Dad says you went riding. I hope you're at the barn . . . call me.

Mom: Okay, that wasn't much really. I'm sorry if I panicked. Just text me when you get these messages so I know you're okay, please?

I texted her a quick thumbs-up and a smiley face so she could relax.

"Hey, you want to stop at Chips and Dairy? It's a block from my house, and they have cheap ice cream. Also, really good poutine." I couldn't oversell the place.

"Sure."

We pulled into the little parking lot at the back of what looked like a small yellow cottage. Once we had our meals, we sat at a picnic table by the play structure.

"My mom used to bring Jake and me here when we were little. They've upgraded the play structure and the patio since then."

"This is a cool place. And this poutine is fantastic," Levi said, forking huge bites of fries, gravy and melting cheese curds into his mouth.

"I know, right?" I said, doing the same.

When we were finished, we sat there, soaking up the sun and enjoying the fullness in our bellies after an eventful day.

"Hey," I said, not sure how to ask him what I wanted to.

"Yeah?"

"So, how come you were in foster care, if you don't mind me asking? You don't have to tell me if you don't want to."

Levi looked into the distance at the stores across Bank Street, and I waited silently for him to either answer the question or deflect it.

"My mom died when I was a baby, and my dad couldn't handle being a single father. That's about the gist of it."

I knew there was more to that story, but I didn't push him.

"It must have been tough for you."

"Yeah. It was." He looked down at his cola can, then up at me. "It's hard to explain what it feels like to find yourself given over to strangers, knowing that the people who should be keeping you safe just ... can't."

I nodded, trying to show I was listening but not wanting to say anything stupid or hurtful. I felt awkward for the first time with Levi, as if the difference in our past situations couldn't be bridged. But then he smiled.

"Anyway, I was really lucky, and those strangers were the best thing that could have happened to me."

"I'm glad."

We sat there enjoying the sunshine and our companionship in quiet contemplation until Levi stood and took our cans to the recycle bin.

"I should get you back."

I sighed. "I guess. You know you're going to have to either match this or exceed it for our next date?"

He laughed and shook his head. "Oh, no. The next one's on you."

"Oh damn."

When Levi pulled his car up to the curb by my house, I wasn't sure if I was supposed to go for a kiss or just say goodbye, so I took off my seatbelt and grabbed the door handle.

But Levi reached out and put his hand on my wrist. "Wait."

I turned. "Huh?"

"I had, like, the best time. And . . . " he glanced out the window, then back at me. "I'm pretty sure if we kiss again, a storm won't come out of nowhere."

"Promise?" I said, leaning toward him. "I probably taste of poutine."

"So do I, so we're even."

Levi was right. It didn't start to thunder, but a sudden burst of lightning hit me all over. We were both breathing hard when we pulled apart.

"Okay, wow," I said.

He grinned. "Yeah. Maybe we did cause that downburst."

I laughed and opened the door. "See ya. Thanks for the awesome first date, Levi."

"Bye. Thanks for all your help in the barn, Dan."

I tried to school my features into a neutral expression before going inside, but failed miserably.

"You had a good time, I can tell!" my mom said when she saw me, as she tried to quiet the dog. "Izzy! My God, stop it."

"Meh, it was okay." There was no way I was going to let on exactly how much fun I'd had.

"How was the riding?" My Dad asked.

"Did you get caught in the storm?" Mom asked.

"Great, and yeah, we did." I shrugged my shoulders as if it hadn't been a big deal. "Got a little wet."

Then I remembered playing with Levi in the stream and kissing him, and I couldn't stop my smile from emerging.

"Levi's a cool guy," I said.

"You volunteered for a worthy cause when you met him at the school. Maybe this is the Universe's way of saying thank you."

"The world doesn't work that way, Mom."

"Maybe it does. Don't look a gift Universe in the mouth," she said, as the dog jumped on me and started yelping again.

"You're hilarious. Jesus, Izzy, would you relax?"

"This dog," my mom said. "I swear to God, next time we're getting a different breed."

"We're not getting another dog," my dad said. "This is it."

"Hmm. You say that now." Mom smiled.

"Izzy's awesome. Just loud," I said, defending him.

"I know, right?" Jake said, looking up from his spot on the couch. "They act like he's so terrible, then when we're not looking, they're giving him kisses and cuddles."

I laughed. "So true."

"He's a little more than we bargained for, that's all," Dad said. "As are the two of you."

"Very funny," I said.

As we sat down to eat the baked pasta my dad had made, I told them all about the horses, and the ranch, and sheltering during the storm. I didn't tell them how safe and protected I'd felt in Levi's arms or how exciting it had been to kiss him in the water.

After supper was over, I went up to my room and FaceTimed Tara.

"Heyo," I said, when she appeared on my screen.

"Oh my God! Don't tell me! You're no longer a virgin!"

"Har har. I'm still a virgin."

She screamed. "FOR NOW!"

"My parents can probably hear you. You know how small this house is?"

"So? Where did Levi take you?"

I told Tara about the ranch.

"What the hell? Levi is a prince among men. And among women, if I'm going to be honest. Jules has never taken me horseback riding. I don't think she even *likes* horses."

"It was fun. He's . . . really awesome."

"Dan, I am so, so happy for you!"

"Oh, and Tara? I've decided I'm nonbinary and I'd like you guys to use they/them for me from now on. If that's okay."

"Dan, that's amazing. Of course, we will. You know that."

"I know. Thank you. You're the best."

"Well, I can't compete with Levi!"

"You don't have to. There are eight different kinds of love, according to the Greeks."

"You don't say. Did your boyfriend tell you that?"

"No, I already knew that. So, Philia is affectionate love, which I have for you in spades. And also Storge, which is familial love. Because we've known each other for so long, you feel like family."

"Aw! Dan! I feel the same way." She grinned wickedly. "And what kind of love do you and Levi have?"

"Eros, definitely. I don't think I need to define that one. And Ludus — playful love. So playful."

"That's a great sign. If he's comfortable enough to be playful, he's definitely feeling you."

* * *

Sunday morning, Levi texted to say he couldn't wait to see me on Monday. I texted back that I felt the same. My thumbs hovered for a second before I added: **u want to watch my vocal solo if u can get out of class?**

While I waited for his response, my pulse skyrocketed, and I almost regretted it. Maybe I'd overestimated his affection for me. Watching someone perform a required assignment for a class you weren't even in was going above and beyond.

Levi: yes pls

Relief overtook me.

Me: yay

Levi: <3

I grinned stupidly and texted a heart back.

I had taken the advice of my music teacher and not practised my solo since the day before. While my parents and Jake had gone to the mall, I had warmed up with some standard vocal exercises and gone through it two times. My voice had been strong and steady, and I had hit all the notes with ease.

I hoped things would go just as well today.

19 I'm Yours

I SPENT AN HOUR IN MY ROOM Sunday night figuring out what I wanted to wear for my solo the next day. I had a kick-ass black Lycra pencil skirt that I'd bought to wear to *The Nutcracker* at the NAC in 2019, because apparently, you had to flag feminine at a fancy event if you were AFAB. Which was complete bullshit, but I'd been too fed up to call anyone out about it. And the skirt did fit me well and showed off my ass and legs, two parts of me that I was very proud of, and that I wanted Levi to have a good look at, even though he'd already seen me in my wet underwear.

I also had a pair of plain black pumps that were reasonably comfortable, but when I put them on with the skirt, it didn't feel right. I was planning to wear a *Greta Van Fleet* T-shirt and the brown blazer over it. So only my burgundy Docs would do.

I figured that the gender binary was a load of crap based on no legitimate science. In fact, everything we knew about sex determination and biology seemed to defy it. It was an ancient social construct that needed to be minimized, if not eliminated altogether. But I realized that would be a hard sell to traditionalists.

I didn't sleep well, because even though my teacher assured me I was ready to perform, I kept thinking about all the things that could go wrong.

My dad wished me luck as he left for the office, and my mom gave me a hug and her best wishes and said she was proud of me for "stepping out of my comfort zone."

"What if I fall flat on my face, though?"

"Those boots look pretty sturdy."

I couldn't tell if that was a compliment or some shade about my choice of footwear, but I smiled and left the house feeling like there was at least a chance I could do this.

My friends on the bus were suitably impressed with my look, which built up my confidence further, and I was relieved to see Levi standing by my locker when I got to school. I congratulated myself silently on choosing to wear the Docs, because they made me feel strong and sexy in the skirt and the rest of it. I'd given them a bit of a polish so they were shiny and sharp.

"Oh, wow," he said, his eyes going comically wide. "You look . . . unbelievably hot. Holy shit, Dan."

I'd gelled my hair into an artfully disorganized mess and put on some black eyeliner, my only concession to wearing makeup.

"Thanks," I said, looking him over. Levi was wearing a snug black long-sleeved shirt that hung past his hips and purple jeans that seemed painted on. "I approve of your fashion choices also."

He reached out and touched my cheek. "I'd kiss you, but everyone is looking."

"So?" I said, because I didn't give a damn.

He smiled and leaned forward as I moved in to meet him.

There were some whoops and off-colour comments, but the kiss grounded me and made the swirling in my stomach lessen.

"See you in second-period. Music class is in room 144," I said when we separated.

"I'll be there."

* * *

Five students had yet to perform. I was third on the list, which turned out to be fortunate since Levi didn't get to the music room until a quarter past the hour. He arrived looking stressed and apologetic, but he waved and gave me a big smile and a thumbs-up.

I was glad he was there, but my anxiety had increased as I'd watched my classmates do so well.

Finally, it was my turn.

"All right," Miss Jacobs said. "Dan is performing 'I'm Yours' by Jason Mraz."

She waved me forward, and I took my place by the piano. I hadn't told Levi what song I had chosen, and I didn't want to look at him, because I didn't want any distractions.

I took a deep breath as Miss Jacobs played the beginning notes on the piano. I pushed all thoughts of the audience out of my head and concentrated on my voice and the lyrics.

It was a song about not wasting time, and in the end, it rang pretty close to home to what I was feeling in terms of Levi and everything we had talked about, and also to taking a chance on a relationship with him.

I stared at a spot on the wall where an LGBTQ2S+ poster hung as I started off with a couple of wobbles. My gaze flicked to Miss Jacobs and her encouraging smile gave me what I needed to recover. The next bit was stronger, and by the time I was into the chorus, I had it.

When it was over and the piano notes died away, there was a stunned silence. Then the room burst into applause.

I finally looked at Levi. He was shaking his head, like he could not believe what he had just witnessed, and clapping as he smiled.

My teacher stood up.

"Well done! That was fantastic, Dan. See? All that hard work paid off."

I would never be a famous singer. I might never sing in public again. But it had been glorious. And everyone seemed surprised by the power of my voice. It was, literally, the best experience I'd ever had within the walls of this place.

"I couldn't have done it without your support, Miss Jacobs."

I moved toward Levi. On my way, people whispered words of praise.

Levi put his arm around me and kissed me when I got there.

"That was amazing," he said. "You are amazing. I

love that song."

I shrugged. "It seemed right."

"It was perfect."

We went to find Tara and Jules once the class was over, since it was lunch.

"Sorry I showed up late," Levi said. "We had a supply and it took some convincing for him to let me leave. I was going to, either way, but I'm glad he realized it was important and I wasn't trying to scam him."

"Oh, geez. I'm glad you got there in time."

"Me, too," he said, steering me toward Tara and Jules. They were waving from a table in the corner of the cafeteria.

"I wish we'd met sooner," I said. "You won't even be here next fall."

He gave me a look, like he didn't understand what I was talking about.

"I'll meet you every day for lunch if you don't get sick of me. My time will be my own, except for the nights I'm working. And on those days, my shifts won't start until three. Speaking of which, I want to take you there."

"There she is!" Tara screamed and jumped up from her spot on the bench beside Jules.

"Whoa," I said, as she grabbed me in a bear hug. I looked at Levi. "Help?"

He laughed but didn't offer any assistance.

"Everybody's talking about you, Dan! News of your solo has preceded you. You're a freaking legend!"

"Um, thanks. This is Levi. Levi, this is Tara. And her girlfriend, Jules."

"What up?" Jules said to Levi, observing Tara's exuberance with affection. "Sorry. She gets excited when she's happy."

"No worries. I get excited all the time."

"I heard," Jules said, waggling her eyebrows.

"I didn't tell them anything," I protested.

Levi sat on the bench opposite Jules and extended his hand.

"Pleased to meet you, Jules."

"You as well. Don't worry," she said, glancing at me and Tara. "They'll be done in a minute."

Tara let me go and lunged toward Levi. "So glad to finally meet you!" she said, shoving her hand at him.

"Easy. Down girl," I said.

"Oh, he's hot."

"Tara!"

"It's true, though," Jules said, as Levi blushed. "Even I can see that. And I'm as hardcore lesbo as they come." She winked at Levi. "And believe me, they do."

He snorted.

"Okay, okay, that's enough, you two. Leave my poor boyfriend alone."

"No, no. Do go on," Levi said, making room for me on the bench. "What are we all eating today?" he asked, opening his backpack and taking out a container.

Jules held up her sandwich. "PB and J."

Tara opened her container. "Garden salad with tuna."

"Dan?" Levi asked, waving his container under my nose. It was full of tasty-looking dolmades.

"I've got chicken salad," I said, gazing at the container and licking my lips. "But I'd love a taste of your dolmades."

Levi smiled as Tara and Jules lost their composure and collapsed with laughter.

We exchanged a glance that held all the promise of the universe.

ACKNOWLEDGEMENTS

I need to thank my wonderful husband, Greg, and my parents, Chris and Charlotte, for encouraging me to write, even when I thought it would never take me anywhere but my own imagination.